The deep blue of his eyes stirred her memory. They were just as she remembered: blue as the Caribbean Sea, and caressing her soul as if she splashed in their seductive depths.

God, she'd missed him—hadn't realized just how much until this moment. She wanted to wrap her arms around him and tell him how rarely a day went by that she didn't think of him, and that never had just seeing someone caused so much mayhem to her mind and body.

The whole package appealed, drew her in. The spark that flickered through her when his warm fingers clasped hers. The heat in his eyes when their gazes met. The way she'd instantly wanted him with an intensity she'd never experienced before or since that spring break they'd met.

She sighed, reminding herself that the first day on her new job wasn't the time or the place to be fantasizing about the hunky doctor who'd haunted her heart for ten years. Or to be rehashing all the reasons why that particular fantasy wouldn't ever come true.

Janice Lynn has a Masters in Nursing from Vanderbilt University, and works as a nurse practitioner in a family practice. She lives in the southern United States with her husband, their four children, their Jack Russell—appropriately named Trouble—and a lot of unnamed dust bunnies that have moved in since she started her writing career. To find out more about Janice and her writing, visit www.janicelynn.com

Recent titles by the same author:

THE HEART SURGEON'S SECRET SON
THE DOCTOR'S PREGNANCY BOMBSHELL

THE DOCTOR'S MEANT-TO-BE MARRIAGE

BY
JANICE LYNN

MILLS & BOON®
Pure reading pleasure™

All the characters in this book have no existence outside
the imagination of the author, and have no relation
whatsoever to anyone bearing the same name or names.
They are not even distantly inspired by any individual
known or unknown to the author, and all the incidents
are pure invention.

First published in Great Britain 2008
Large Print edition 2008
Harlequin Mills & Boon Limited,
Eton House, 18-24 Paradise Road,
Richmond, Surrey TW9 1SR

ISBN: 978 0 263 19991 8

Set in Times Roman 16¾ on 19 pt.
17-1108-45112

Printed and bound in Great Britain
by Antony Rowe Ltd, Chippenham, Wiltshire

THE DOCTOR'S
MEANT-TO-BE
MARRIAGE

CHAPTER ONE

DR CHELSEA MAJORS pulled on her lab coat and prepared to bask in the first day of the rest of her life.

OK, so maybe she was being overly dramatic, but she'd worked a long time to get to this particular morning. Today she started work at Madison Medical Center, a family clinic that employed three physicians. Make that, as of today, four.

She'd never considered going anywhere other than the moderate-sized practice near Alabama's Gulf Shore coast where her brother worked. From the time of her birth Will had practically raised her. Certainly, she'd spent a lot more time in his care than her parents'.

Henry and Iva Majors had had lives to save,

extended overseas mission trips to go on, and medical boards to run. Dealing with their youngest child had been left to hired help. Chelsea had preferred the care of her nanny to her often times indifferent parents anyway. Will had been another story. He'd been the perfect son while Chelsea had been an accident from the moment of conception. Her mother had had no qualms at pointing out that due to her difficult pregnancy she'd had to miss out on an important mission trip to Bosnia.

Plus, she was pretty sure her parents had decided a mistake had been made at the hospital and they'd been given the wrong child. Who could blame them when they were such overachievers? Her father, her mother, her brother. Everyone but her.

For too many years she'd been stuck inside her defective body and an outcast within her own home. Will had been able to go with their parents on their overseas trips, to live their lives. Chelsea's medical problems had kept her at home, in the care of others, and somewhere along the line she and her parents had missed forming loving bonds.

But with Will's encouragement and her own determination, she'd come past all that and achieved her lifelong dream of becoming a family physician. She wanted to make a difference in others' lives the way a few good doctors had in hers. Not by serving on some politically connected health board or by going overseas, but to make a difference in a small-town community that would likely never earn her any commendations from the president. Her parents already had enough of those hanging on the wall.

"You ready, sis?" a tall, dark-haired male version of herself asked. Will stepped into the closet-sized room she couldn't be more proud of—her office—and tossed a small package to her.

"What's this?" Examining the gold foil and white silk ribbon, she held up the square gift-wrapped box. She met her brother's twinkling brown eyes, so similar to her own. Her heart pinched at his thoughtfulness. Although seven years her senior, they'd always been close and she admitted to hero-worshipping him for as long as she could remember. Will had been her hero, making her believe in herself when it would have been too easy to shut the world out.

"Just a little something to let you know how proud I am of my kid sister," he said, prowling through the cardboard box on her desk. He lifted a small, stuffed bear in doctor garb, curled his nose, then dropped the fuzzy animal back into the box. "I thought we got your stuff moved in on Saturday?"

The bear had been a gift from a group of under-grad friends in celebration of when she'd gotten her acceptance letter to medical school. She cherished the gift, just as she cherished the friend-ships. Having been homeschooled with very little interaction with others until her teens, she never took for granted the blessing of having friends.

"Almost everything." She glanced at the bookshelf with her precious medical books lined up in neat rows. Nodding toward the box, she said, "This is personal stuff to give the room my personality."

Will's handsome face wrinkled in a look of thorough disgust. "You're going to make this room all girly," he teased.

She rolled her eyes and finished unwrapping his gift. Her eyes misted at what she saw nestled in the tissue paper.

"Oh, Will. You shouldn't have." She wrapped her arms around him and gave an appreciative squeeze. "Have I told you lately that you're my favorite brother?"

"I'm your only brother," he reminded her, indulgently hugging her with a pleased grin on his face. "Give it here so I can pin it on your lab coat."

She handed him the name tag he'd had made for her, one printed with her name and the name of the practice. He pinned the tag to her white lab coat and studied her appearance, much as he'd done many times throughout her childhood.

The badge was a cheap piece of plastic, but the love behind the gift was priceless. Will knew how hard she'd worked, how she'd longed for this day.

Not all the reasons she'd longed for it, of course.

Because her brother didn't know about the passionate kiss she'd shared with Jared ten years ago.

Neither did Will know how excited she was at the fact his partner was going to be a daily part of her life.

The truth was, though, she also dreaded seeing Jared, of having to constantly face the man who haunted her dreams when she knew she could never have him. When her ex's rejection had left her emotionally doubled over, she could only imagine what seeing the disgust in Jared's eyes, hearing him say she was unlovable would do to her poor heart. No, she wouldn't open herself up to the kind of pain Jared had the power to deliver. Never again. She'd offered her heart to him on a platter and he'd turned her away, asked another woman to marry him, driving the message home that she hadn't been good enough.

Oblivious to her thoughts of the past, Will straightened the name tag, and shook his head slightly. A look of pride shone in his golden brown eyes. "There, you look perfect."

Reminding herself of all she'd accomplished, of the life she'd forged for herself, Chelsea bit back an ironic laugh. Perfect? If only.

Dr Jared Floyd read over Connie Black's MRI report, not liking the radiologist's comments. He'd hoped arthritis had been causing her worsening hip pain, but according to the report a tumor was growing in the sixty-year-old woman's left hip joint.

Which meant he had to deliver the bad news at Connie's appointment in the morning. Damn.

Connie had come so far from three years ago when he'd first diagnosed her lung cancer. She'd quit smoking, survived the removal of one of her right lung lobes, endured chemotherapy and radiation, and suffered through the loss of her husband three months ago to a massive heart attack. She'd endured everything and kept a positive outlook. Now this.

He stared at the report, hoping the wording would change.

Highly suspicious mass with solid consistency and increased vascularization. Biopsy recommended.

Maybe the radiologist was wrong.

Maybe he was doing a lot of wishful thinking.

And definitely a whole lot of procrastinating.

Sighing, he left the report on his desk and went to examine his patients. Normally, he cleared up lab and radiology reports before starting his appointments and usually he finished quickly. Today, he'd tarried.

Partially due to Connie's bad MRI report, but also because of the clinic's newest employee.

Chelsea. He'd avoided seeing her since the night he'd made the biggest mistake of his life. Not an easy task when she was his best friend's little sister. Today his avoidance would come to a screeching halt because, with Chelsea joining the practice, he'd see her more days than not.

How could he remain faithful to Laura's memory if he was constantly confronted with the woman who'd made him second-guess his heart?

Knowing he had to get the inevitable over with, he headed to her office just in time to hear Will's teasing.

"Now," Chelsea's brother said, "go see your patients before I have to fire you for slacking on the job. Nepotism will get you nowhere around here."

Yeah, right. Will babied his kid sister and wouldn't even consider Chelsea going to work elsewhere when Jared, risking his friend's anger, had voiced his concerns. Family and business didn't mix. Too bad Will had ignored Jared's less than subtle hints.

"Oh," Chelsea said as she rounded the corner of her office doorway, bumping into him. Surprised golden brown eyes lifted, met his and she gave a sharp, surprised gasp. "Jared."

Reflexively, he grasped her arms to steady her and was struck by a hauntingly familiar waft of something sweet, like homemade cookies or vanilla. Whatever the fragrance, the inviting smell filled him with the desire to take a deep breath. Just as the thought of knowing only the cotton fabric of her lab coat separated their skins filled him with the memory of the single kiss they'd shared and how he'd run his hands over her bare arms that night.

She'd been so beautiful, so full of life, so innocent. Yet the sparks between them had been anything but when she'd caught him off guard by pressing her body to his. By pressing her lips to his.

Even now he recalled the warmth of her lips, the moan that had escaped her mouth when he'd kissed her back, the softness of her flesh when he'd molded her to him.

God, he hadn't been able to get close enough, hadn't been able to stop himself from kissing her even though he'd known it had been wrong. He'd have sold his soul that night to have made love to Chelsea.

And although he'd gotten his body under control before they'd done much more than kiss, he hadn't walked away with his soul intact. Far from it.

No, kissing Chelsea had cost him a great deal, too much.

Which he didn't need to be thinking of because some things were best forgotten.

Not that he'd been able to forget, despite years of trying.

Some things truly were unforgettable.

"Jared," she repeated, her gaze traveling over him, almost as if she couldn't resist seeing how time had changed him. Her honey-colored gaze softened, almost becoming a caress, stroking his insides to an ooey-gooey mess. Red stained her cheeks when her eyes lifted to his and she realized what she'd done. "It's been a long time."

His heart thudded against his chest in a rapid beat and his bones turned to jelly, leaving him off-kilter. Had he secretly wondered what Chelsea would think of him after all this time? Of how she'd perceive the changes the years had etched on him?

Annoyed at her stirring of his senses and thoughts, he frowned. How could he want to lean in and get a better smell of a woman he didn't even want to like?

"Yes, it has." *Too long. Not long enough.* "I was on my way to say hello," he said matter-of-factly to cover his slip.

She smiled, flashing perfect white teeth. Her mouth made him think of his favorite female actress, of her classic, infectious smile. Wide, bright, and contagious. Despite his determination to remain impassive, outwardly at least, her smile made his lips want to curve upward.

Which only served to annoy him all the more.

Although she was older than the too-young-for-him seventeen she'd been when they'd first met, there were a thousand reasons why he needed to stay away from Chelsea and safeguard himself from getting close to her. Even if she did now work at Madison Medical Center.

Chelsea held out her hand. She had nice hands with slender fingers and clean, unpainted nails.

Unable to avoid the greeting, Jared clasped

the hand of the girl who'd become a woman in the years since he'd last seen her.

Warm. Electric.

His blood sizzled and fried his brain, short-circuiting the logic that said he shouldn't think Chelsea's soft touch so compelling, her smell so mesmerizing, her nearness so seductive. Time hadn't changed the way she heated his blood. Unfortunately.

He let go of her hand, wondering why he wanted to turn her hand over and run his fingers over her palm. Ridiculous. He wasn't a romantic and even if he had been, Chelsea would be the last person on his list of possible valentines. She held the power to destroy everything he held dear.

Their gazes met and desire flickered in her eyes. Desire he'd last seen right before she'd kissed him ten years ago.

At seventeen she'd affected his libido more than any other woman before or since. She'd also left him feeling guiltier than at any other point in his life.

Foolish as the notion was, he'd thought avoiding her would protect him.

He'd learned the hard way not to tempt fate and Chelsea tempted in too many ways.

"Ahem." Will cleared his throat from behind his sister.

First shooting Jared a dazzling smile, Chelsea scowled at her brother. "Hold your 'taters."

"My 'taters, huh?" Will laughed, giving his sister a conspiratorial wink. "That's a new name for them. But if you insist on my holding them…"

"Eww." She rolled her eyes. "Keep your nastiness to yourself, please." Seeming glad of the interruption, she sighed with great exaggeration. "Do you have a brother, Jared?" she asked. "Because, if not, you're welcome to mine."

"Hey, what happened to being your favorite brother?" Will asked, pretending to be hurt.

"Like you said, you're my only brother. Which means you're also my least favorite." Obviously relaxed in her brother's presence, she grinned mischievously. "Now, quit pestering me at work. I've got patients to see."

With that she paused long enough to bestow another uncertain glance on Jared, swished her ponytail with a great deal of sass at her brother, and headed toward the exam rooms.

"Isn't she something?" Will asked with obvious indulgence.

Not sure how he was supposed to answer, Jared opted for watching Chelsea pause outside the first exam room. Why did she hesitate? Had their reunion left her as shaken as he found himself? Was she recalling how their mouths had felt against each other, how she'd moaned, parted her lips beneath his, granting him sweet surrender?

He winced. Her reasons didn't matter because Jared planned to keep his distance. No matter that he found himself wanting to lean in and inhale her seductive scent, to know if she still tasted heavenly, to know everything there was to discover.

He turned and found Will watching him with narrowed eyes.

"She's off-limits."

Jared snorted. Despite the way he'd once again responded to Chelsea, he didn't need this particular warning. "It's not like that."

"Uh-uh." Will didn't look convinced. He pulled him inside Chelsea's small office. "You're one of my partners and best friends." Will's eyes lost the good-natured humor that usually shone there, replaced by a steel Jared had never seen in his pal's gaze. "But my sister is not your type."

Recall of the electricity that had short-circuited his brain reminded him that physically Chelsea was exactly his type, but he kept his mouth shut. He was above acting on physical attraction when that attraction came in the form of something so bad for him.

"No problem." He spoke slowly, keeping his voice level. "Because I don't date coworkers anyway."

Particularly one who was his partner's baby sister and would turn his life totally upside down if he wasn't careful.

He'd already been through that scenario once and didn't care for an encore.

CHAPTER TWO

CHELSEA paused outside the exam room door and closed her eyes, welcoming Jared's image into her mind.

The deep blue of his eyes stirred her memory. They were just as she remembered them, as blue as the Caribbean Sea and caressing her soul as if she splashed in their seductive depths.

In stark contrast to his eyes was the midnight inkiness of his hair, hair that promised silky smoothness beneath her fingertips. She'd itched to reach out and touch a strand, to see if his hair was really as soft as she recalled. His cheekbones were high, his chin strong with a tiny cleft in the center. Jared's slightly crooked nose added character, making her think he'd probably broken it as a mischievous little boy.

God, she'd missed him, hadn't realized just how much until this moment. She wanted to wrap her arms around him and tell him how rarely a day went by that she didn't think of him, and that never had just seeing someone caused so much chaos to her mind and body.

But her attraction to Jared ran much deeper than the surface. For all his good looks, she'd met more handsome men and not felt the flutters still dancing in her belly.

The whole package appealed, drew her in.

The way he smelled spicy clean. The spark that flickered through her when his warm fingers clasped hers. The heat in his eyes when their gazes met. The way she'd instantly wanted him with an intensity she'd never experienced before or since that spring break they'd met.

She'd looked at him and seen her future.

She'd seen…

Chelsea! Get a grip. Her hot thoughts meant allowing someone to see the Chelsea she kept carefully hidden away from the world, and that's something she'd only done once. The result hadn't been pretty, and she never wanted to bare her scars again.

Yet, realistically, she knew that to marry and have children, which she hoped to do someday, she'd eventually have to trust someone to see the real her.

She sighed, reminding herself the first day on her new job wasn't the time or the place to be fantasizing about the hunky doctor who'd haunted her heart for ten years. Or to be re-hashing all the reasons why that particular fantasy wouldn't ever come true.

Taking a steadying breath, she knocked on the door and entered the exam room.

With tachycardia, bulging eyes, and rapid weight loss, her first patient probably suffered from hyperthyroidism. After giving him a complete examination she gave a lab slip to the nurse and asked him to schedule a follow-up appointment for a few days hence.

Chelsea washed her hands and went to the next patient room to read the chart notation.

Five patients later, and feeling good about her morning, she stood outside an exam room, reviewing the nurse's note. *Hannah Belew. Sixteen. Wants to go on oral contraceptive.*

"Hi, Hannah."

The petite young woman on the exam table didn't appear to be in her teens, much less like she should be asking for birth control. However, Chelsea refrained from pointing out her observation as the girl already looked like her hackles were up.

"The nurse's note says you'd like to discuss birth control. I'll need to ask some questions so you and I can decide together which birth-control option is the most appropriate for you."

"OK," the girl said with a pink tinge to her cheeks. She didn't meet Chelsea's gaze.

"Have you ever had a pelvic examination before?"

Mouth agape, the girl shook her head. "No way."

"Are you sexually active?"

She hesitated, giving Chelsea her answer.

"You won't tell my mom any of this? Patient confidentiality and all that, right?"

A sticky question if ever there was one.

"I'm not obligated to tell as long as you're not threatening your life or someone else's."

"I have a boyfriend," Hannah admitted, apparently satisfied with Chelsea's response. The young girl shrugged her shoulders. "He likes sex."

"Do you?" Chelsea asked the obvious question, catching the teenager off guard.

"Like sex?" Hannah averted her eyes and took a moment before answering. "I like my boyfriend."

Apparently Chelsea wasn't the only one who could answer with diplomacy.

"Hannah, if your boyfriend really cares about you, he'd like you regardless of whether or not you agree to have sex."

Regardless of whether or not long scars marred your back.

Kevin hadn't, and Chelsea often wondered if the scars from his rejection ran deeper than those of the surgeons who'd operated on her scoliosis.

Then again, Jared had also rejected her, without having seen the imperfections of her body. But she'd understood, even respected his determination to do the right thing as she'd been underage.

Hannah didn't speak, but Chelsea could feel walls being thrown up. The young girl didn't want to hear what needed to be said.

"At your age," Chelsea continued, "abstinence is most often the wisest choice, but, regardless, sex is an important step in a relationship. Both parties should be ready for that step and should enjoy making that step when the time arrives."

"He didn't force me," Hannah said pointedly.

"Perhaps you were ready for that step," Chelsea continued gently, "but perhaps you weren't and only went along with what your boyfriend wanted because you were afraid of losing him."

Hannah's lower lip disappeared into her mouth and the girl squirmed on the exam table, crinkling the protective paper covering the vinyl top.

"It's my job to help you take care of your health. That means your mental and emotional health as well as your physical."

"I'm not sick," Hannah insisted. "I just want to go on the Pill so I won't get pregnant."

"Even if you go on the Pill, you still need to make your boyfriend wear a condom. The only way to protect yourself from sexually transmitted diseases is to abstain or have your partner wear a condom."

"Or to have sex with a virgin," Hannah added with a touch of irritation. "I know all this already. We went over this stuff during health class when I was in junior high school." She eyed Chelsea suspiciously. "You're going to tell my mom, aren't you?"

"No, but I recommend you tell her."

"Me tell her? You have got to be kidding me." The girl snorted, her expression dramatic. "I thought you said your job was to look out for my health, not to get me killed."

"Your mom wouldn't kill you."

"Maybe not," Hannah admitted. "But she wouldn't let me see Brett anymore, and that's worse than dying."

Having fallen hard for Jared at only a year older than Hannah, Chelsea wouldn't judge the girl. Neither would she point out that her entire life was ahead of her, whether Brett remained in her life or not.

"Whether or not you tell your mother is your choice. My job is to give you the best information I can so you can make wise health-care decisions. In this case, having an open discussion with your mother is what I believe to be best."

Ha, like she'd ever had an open discussion with her own mother. These days, she and Iva only saw each other a couple of times a year. Thank God, as she didn't think she could survive more. Only through Will did Chelsea find contact with her parents tolerable. Sometimes she wondered if they would even include her in family activities if not for her brother.

What right did she have to advise Hannah to tell her mother? What if Hannah's mother made Iva look warm and cuddly?

"It's your call," she said softly. "But I want you to at least consider talking with her."

"Sure." Sarcasm never dripped as thickly as it did off Hannah's flippant tongue.

Chelsea took a deep breath. She didn't seem to be getting through to the teenager.

"OK, let's move on. We'll discuss the different birth-control options you have."

Hannah's gaze narrowed. "What kind of options?"

"Pill, patch, shot, cervical cap, intra-uterine device, all of which require a pelvic examination first."

The girl cringed. "You have to see me down there?"

"To do the thin prep test that checks your cervical and vaginal cells, I have to physically examine you."

The girl's face fell. "I don't think I can do that."

"Have a pelvic exam?" Chelsea clarified,

wanting to make sure she understood what Hannah was saying.

The girl nodded. "Just the thought embarrasses me and makes my skin feel hot and sweaty."

"You have to have the test before I will write you any type of prescription birth control."

Hannah let out a long sigh. "Why?"

"Some tumors grow at an accelerated rate when hormones are added."

Hannah rolled her eyes. "I don't need hormones. I just want the Pill so I don't get pregnant."

"Many types of birth control are hormones, including the Pill."

"Oh." The girl sat quietly, digesting what Chelsea had told her.

"Another thing you should consider having is the HPV vaccine."

The girl crossed her arms and gave Chelsea a smug look. "I've had all my vaccines."

"That's wonderful, and perhaps you have had HPV, too, but it isn't a required vaccine so not everyone has. The vaccine is recommended for girls aged nine through twenty-six. HPV, or human papillomavirus, is the most common sexually transmitted disease in the United States and causes most cases of cervical cancer."

Hannah's eyes became round. "There's an STD that causes cancer?"

"Yes." Chelsea was glad to see she'd caught the girl's interest. "There are around fifty strands of the virus. The vaccine protects against the strands causing cervical cancer."

"If this HDP is so common, why haven't I ever heard of it?"

"HPV, and you probably have heard of the disease without knowing it. Genital warts are also caused by human papillomavirus," she explained.

Hannah's nose curled in disgust, and she nodded. "I do remember studying those during health class. Nasty business."

"Let me give you some information to read." Feeling pleased she'd made a connection with the girl, Chelsea stood. "I'll come back in a few minutes, and you can decide what you'd like to do regarding your pelvic examination and the vaccine."

She stepped into the hallway and didn't see Betty anywhere. Scanning the nurses' station, she wondered where brochures and handouts might be kept but didn't see anywhere obvious.

"Problems?" a deep voice asked from behind her. A voice belonging to the man she'd had to force off her mind all morning. Her spirits lifted just at knowing he was near, that he still felt the connection between them and had sought an excuse to search her out, to share a conversation. Perhaps he was a man confident enough to overlook her imperfections and care for her just as she was. Hey, a girl could dream.

She turned, but her heart stalled.

Jared's eyes would have formed glaciers on the sun. Ouch. Why was he looking at her like that? With something akin to… Chelsea sought the right word and could only come up with loathing.

But he couldn't loathe her. All she'd done had been to ineptly flirt with him ten years ago. OK, she'd kissed him, too, but he'd kissed her back, so surely he didn't blame that completely on her?

Jared had left the next day and, despite initially trying to contact him, she'd not seen him since.

Not knowing how she'd clung to his words, Will had updated her from time to time. Jared wasn't married and, other than the longtime girlfriend she hadn't known about when they'd first met, there hadn't been anyone special in his life. Laura. She'd suffered at the name, mourned at the existence of the woman who had held Jared's heart, but she'd never wished the girl's fate on her. Later that same year Laura had been killed in a car accident.

Jared was Will's best friend. He wouldn't hold a grudge for ten years over something as simple as her foolishly throwing herself at him. Would he?

Wishing she didn't feel like she carried the bubonic plague, she gave a slight smile. "I was looking for a handout on the HPV vaccine and hoping we had one that explains pelvic examinations."

Without any softening of his features he pointed to the small lab where basic phlebotomy tests were performed. "In those two filing cabinets."

She nodded, expecting him to walk away, but instead he opened a drawer and pulled out a sheet on the vaccination.

"We keep folders here with all immunization information in them. I don't recall seeing a handout explaining what to expect during a pelvic examination, but if there is one, it would be in here." He flipped through another drawer.

Chelsea stared at the back of his dark head, wishing she could read his thoughts.

"Nothing," he said, closing the drawer and facing her. "You can probably pull something up online when you get time and mail it to your patient."

Good idea, except she didn't think Hannah would be receptive to getting mail at home regarding the reasons for her office visit.

Although she'd verbally gone over what would take place, she wanted Hannah to have something concrete that explained exactly what would happen during the exam.

"Or I have a patient-education program on my computer. It might have something."

"Really?"

"We could check…" He hesitated and she wondered if he regretted his words even before they'd completely left his lips.

"If it wouldn't be a bother."

He didn't meet her eyes. "No bother."

Chelsea followed him to his office, surprised he'd offered when he seemed so antagonistic toward her. Perhaps he was afraid she was going to throw herself at him like she'd done all those years ago. She wouldn't, of course. Sure, being near him gave her those same throw-caution-to-the-wind urges, but she'd matured, gained some experience with the opposite sex. She wouldn't make a fool of herself again.

Jared stood beside his desk and clicked his computer mouse, bringing up the home screen. Chelsea used the moment to glance around his office.

Plain, uncomplicated, and to the point. No personal items other than the award and acknowledgment certificates framed on the wall. Already her office had more of her than this room reflected of its owner.

Then again, maybe he liked keeping things simple and the minimalist look worked for him.

"I've got a couple of different programs, but if we can't find what you need, the Internet is sure to have something."

Chelsea's gaze returned to him, going over the lean lines of his body. Time had been good to Jared. Too good. If possible, she thought he was even more handsome now than he'd been ten years ago, but there was something different, something missing from his eyes. The happy twinkle she'd grown to love that spring break. Instead, Jared's eyes only shone with a deep inner sadness that she suspected many failed to see.

"I appreciate this," she said, swallowing the

lump in her throat. She had to stop thinking of Jared as a martyr or as a pinup poster. Just because he looked like a brooding pinup model, it didn't give her the right to keep mentally ogling him. Wasn't that what women were known to complain about happening to them? Personally, Chelsea could go for a little visual ogling from time to time, just to boost her battered ego, but she digressed.

Jared was her colleague, her coworker, and her brother's best friend. For her to embarrass them both by throwing herself at him again would just be wrong. Plus, her attraction to him would make their professional relationship strained. She'd worked too hard to get her degree, to have the career she dreamed of, to let misplaced hormones rob her future.

"Ah." He glanced over his shoulder to indicate she should check out what he'd pulled up on his computer monitor. "This what you're looking for?"

Chelsea skimmed the form. "Perfect."

He clicked the mouse again, and the page shot

out of his printer. "Here. If you run across some-thing else you need and can't find it, let me know. Patient education is important."

"Yes." She took the offered printout and glanced at it without really seeing the diagrams and words. "Thank you, Jared."

"You're welcome." An awkward moment passed where they stared at each other, not speaking, just locking gazes. He looked away, swiped his palms over his pants, then closed the computer program. "Got to get back to my patients."

"Right."

They both stepped out into the hallway.

"Oh, there you are!" Leslie, a bubbly nurse practitioner who worked in the clinic, saw Chelsea and bounded up to give her a quick hug. "Sorry I missed you this morning." Her gaze swerved for a second. "I got a late start, but no matter. I've been hoping to catch sight of you all morning." She flashed a smile at Jared. "You, too, actually."

Jared's brow rose, but he didn't comment.

"Will, Jennifer and I want the entire office to go out tonight for dinner to celebrate Chelsea's first day."

Chelsea opened her mouth to say she'd love to, but was frozen in place by Jared's arctic attitude. She inwardly sighed.

"I'm busy," he said.

Fighting frostbite, Chelsea tried not to let his words hurt her. It wasn't as if she'd really expected him to want to have a relationship with her. Sure, she'd dreamed, but in reality even her dreams had only been private fantasies. Even to have a fling with Jared meant baring her soul, her back. Letting someone as beautiful as Jared see her marred flesh was not going to happen.

"Busy?" Leslie's gaze narrowed as she eyed him curiously. "Jennifer is on call for the hospital, but amazingly the rest of us have the evening off. We won't get a better opportunity than this evening for us all to get together, and you know it."

Chelsea could almost see Jared's brain

whirling, trying to get out of the dinner. Did he plan to avoid her as much as possible?

He'd managed quite well over the past ten years and hadn't been there on any of the occasions when she'd visited her brother. He'd even gone out of the country for six weeks during the time she had been officially hired.

"Come on, Jared," Leslie coaxed. "No flavor of the month is more important than business."

Flavor of the month? Heat rushed into Chelsea's cheeks and her fingers gripped the printout she held so tightly the edges crinkled.

The coolness of his gaze covered her skin in goose bumps.

She didn't understand his strange reaction, but refused to slump into negativity or pity. She didn't do either. Hadn't for a long, long time.

He crossed his arms and glared. "Go without me. I'll swing by when I can. Just let me know what restaurant you decide on."

Chelsea didn't believe him. And not just because he talked through gritted teeth. What was his problem?

"Hey, Jare," Will said, rounding the corner with a chart in hand and his nurse closely on his tail. "Leslie fill you in on tonight's plans? We've got to officially celebrate my little sis's induction to the paying workforce."

Leslie's gaze cut to Will and a pretty pink tinted her cheeks, making Chelsea wonder which of the men caused her blush. "I was just telling him, but Jared says he has other plans."

"Cancel." Will shrugged nonchalantly at his friend. "You're going with us tonight."

Chelsea had had enough of feeling like the scraggy puppy in the pet-shop window.

"I'm fine with whatever you decide, but I need to get back to my patient." She waved the printout as if that explained everything and walked away before she went into total embarrassed meltdown. Later, when alone with her thoughts, she'd try to figure out why Jared had acted so oddly. If it was because he thought she was going to make his work environment unpleasant by mooning over him, she'd set him straight.

She'd gotten quite good at keeping her emotions hidden.

Chelsea gave the printout to Hannah for her to look over while she saw another patient. When she'd finished, she returned to Hannah's exam room, but the girl was gone.

"Betty?" She went in search of the nurse. Spotting the pretty, slightly overweight forty-year-old, she asked, "Is Hannah in the restroom?"

Blowing a stray short, dyed-platinum strand of hair out of her eye, Betty gave Chelsea a confused look. "She left."

"Left?"

Betty nodded. "Right after you came out of the exam room, she took off. I thought you'd finished."

Glancing into the room, Chelsea saw the counter and trash bin were both empty. Well, at least Hannah had taken the brochures.

CHAPTER THREE

WHAT had he agreed to?

Nothing. He hadn't agreed, and no way was he going to dinner with Chelsea. Not even with his partners there as buffers. He'd been right to avoid her and should stick with that plan as much as current circumstances allowed.

But for the rest of the day Jared's mind kept drifting back to how his skin had tingled when they'd touched, how her smile gave glimpses of lightheartedness, how his body perked up at her nearness.

But he shouldn't do anything to encourage thoughts that there could ever be anything between them. There couldn't. Attraction between him and Chelsea was the last thing he needed. His life in Madison was good, exactly what he wanted. It had taken him a long time to find happiness after Laura's death and he wouldn't risk losing that hard-won inner peace.

Not peace, really, he had too much guilt for that, would always have too much guilt over what had happened to Laura, but he'd come to terms of a sort with what had happened.

He'd done the right thing, focused on his relationship with Laura when she'd told him she was pregnant the week after she'd returned from Greece. The week after he'd met Chelsea.

Laura had known something had changed, that he hadn't been the same after spring break. She'd pushed, she'd prodded, she'd begged him to tell her if he wanted her to have an abortion. He hadn't, but neither had he been able to admit that he'd fallen for a seventeen-year-old girl. He'd pushed thoughts of Chelsea aside, had asked Laura to marry him, and had committed himself to being a good husband and father.

She'd been ecstatic, until she'd overheard a conversation not meant for her ears. A conversation when his buddies Larry and Tom had ragged him about Chelsea and the way she hero-worshipped him. Jared had snapped, telling them to shut up, but it had been too late. Laura had seen the truth on his face, and they'd argued.

Although not in the way she'd wanted, he had loved Laura and would have done everything in his power to make her happy, would have been a good husband and father.

He'd never gotten the opportunity.

That night, she'd swerved off the rode, hit a tree, and lost their baby and her life.

Guilt had held him captive ever since.

Guilt that said he didn't deserve happiness, particularly not with Chelsea.

"Dr Jared?" interrupted his nurse, Kayla Welker. He'd hired Kayla the month he'd started at the clinic and he'd never had cause to regret his decision.

He blinked, clearing the past from his mind. For the moment, at least. "Yes?"

"Sorry to bother you, but I just put Anthony Rogle in room two. He's wheezing. Do you want me to give him a breathing treatment, or would you like to check him first?"

"I'll see Tony first. Go ahead and set up the nebulizer, though. No doubt, he'll need it." Jared followed Kayla to the exam room where the pale twenty-one-year-old struggled to catch his breath, wheezing audibly. A beautiful girl sat next to him, holding his hand and whispering assurances.

"Thank goodness, Dr Jared." The young woman sighed her relief. "Tony is having another attack."

"Hey, Emily." Jared motioned for Kayla to start the machine as soon as she got the apparatus set up. He listened to Tony's heaving chest. "Any triggering factors this time?"

Emily shook her head. "We were at work, and his chest started heaving. He used his inhaler, but his breathing didn't get better so I drove him here. Doc, why has he started having these attacks? They scare the devil out of me!"

"Quit…talking…about me…like I'm not here," the thin, pale young man ordered, giving his girlfriend an irritated look as he panted for air.

Kayla handed Tony the breathing apparatus, and he began inhaling the albuterol solution via the nebulizer. The noise of the machine droned through the otherwise silent room. When Tony gave the thumbs-up sign that his wheezing was starting to ease, Jared turned to Emily and Kayla.

"Keep an eye on him. I'll be back in a few minutes."

Two months ago Tony had suffered his first asthma attack. He'd had no prior history of problems. His episodes occurred mostly at work, but he'd had a few at home and one at his girlfriend's family home.

His hand-held inhalers helped on occasion, but more and more Tony's attacks weren't eased without a trip into the office or the emergency room. More often than not, getting his attack under control required a steroid injection along with the nebulizer treatment. Jared tried to avoid the steroid shot if possible because of the potential side effects. Hopefully as Tony could already feel some relief, using the nebulizer, no injection would be needed today.

What was causing the young man's attacks?

Developing asthma at twenty-one wasn't a common phenomenon. They'd gone through Tony's risk factors, and although he worked in the paint shop of a boat factory he always wore proper ventilation masks. There had been no new products or changes in the home and he didn't have a pet. There were no recent illnesses and once the attack passed, Tony felt fine except for being tired, a frequent symptom following an asthma attack.

Jared saw his next patient, a schoolteacher needing a refill on her anxiety medication. When he'd finished, he knocked on Tony's door. The nebulizer no longer hummed, meaning the treatment had finished.

"How's the breathing?"

"Much better, Doc," Tony answered, talking without sounding winded. Emily still sat, squeezing his hand and watching him nervously, like she expected his chest to heave again any moment. All that Jared had expected to see. What he hadn't expected to see was Chelsea smiling at his patients, chatting with them while she packed up the nebulizer. What was she doing and where was Kayla?

Chelsea's golden brown gaze met his and for a moment he felt as if she searched his soul, seeking answers to questions he couldn't acknowledge. But then she slid on a professional façade, picked up the machine, and gave a tight smile.

"Kayla had some business to take care of, and I was between patients," she said by way of explanation. Without glancing his way again, she pushed past him in the small room. Her shoulder brushed against his, making his nerve endings pulse to life. Her scent filled his nostrils, making him feel as if he was struggling for his next breath every bit as much as Tony had prior to his treatment.

When she closed the door behind her, he sucked in air, hoping to ease his oxygen-deprived brain cells, or whatever was making him feel so dizzy.

He turned to Tony and Emily. "What happened?"

"I was on break and all of a sudden I couldn't catch my breath. I felt like an elephant was sitting on my chest." Tony placed his hand over his sternum. "Like I needed to rip my rib cage open so air could get into my lungs."

How he'd just felt with Chelsea near.

He winced at the thought and focused on his patient. "You used your inhaler?"

Tony nodded. "I even took more puffs than I'm supposed to, but I just couldn't catch my breath. I should probably take my nebulizer with me to work."

"Are you using your nebulizer often?"

"I've used it some," the young man admitted. "But since you started me on that asthma tablet I've only had to use the machine twice."

"You're using the inhaled steroid, too?"

"Just like you told me."

"You haven't thought of anything that's changed within the past two months?"

"Same house, same car, same job, same girlfriend." Tony shot Emily a teasing glance. "I could replace her and see if she's the problem."

She slapped his arm. "Then you really wouldn't be able to breathe because I'd strangle you."

The tender kiss she placed on his cheek and the worried way she watched each breath he took told another story.

Tony winked. "See what kind of abuse I have to put up with, Doc?"

"I see." Jared smiled at the couple, wondering if he'd ever been that young. He had, of course. He'd foolishly thought he'd been in love and had destroyed much of his life. Destroyed Laura's life. "I'm going to keep you here a while longer just to make sure you're over the attack. I'll have Kayla check on you in a few and if things are OK, we'll let you go home. I'm going to go ahead and set you up to see a pulmonologist, though. That's a lung specialist. Maybe he can figure out what's causing these attacks."

Jared planned to do more research that night to see if he could unravel any clues about why Tony had suddenly started having his attacks.

Although, recalling his dinner plans, his research might be later than he intended.

Darn Will and Leslie for putting him on the spot like that. There'd been no way for him to continue to refuse without raising their suspicions. He didn't want to deal with questions about why he didn't want to go, why he didn't want to be around Chelsea.

He'd call and cancel because being near Chelsea definitely caused *him* breathing problems.

Chelsea brushed her hand over the clean lines of her cherry-wood desk. She glanced approvingly at the gleaming surface, smiling at how her first day had gone.

Other than Hannah Belew, all the patients had seemed to accept her and be pleased with their care. Chelsea was holding out hope that Hannah would schedule her pelvic examination and vaccination. Maybe the girl would decide to go to the local health department. Or decide not to have sex anymore.

And Jared, well, she just didn't know what to

think about his odd reaction. She'd always wondered what he'd say, what he'd do when their paths crossed again. She hadn't expected the coldness. Not really. Maybe a few awkward moments until he realized she wasn't going to launch herself at him, but then he'd laugh and treat her with the same fondness he had that spring.

Only Jared was different in that regard. He looked like he rarely laughed these days. Had Laura's death robbed him of that inner joy Chelsea had found so charismatic?

"What are you looking so contrite about?" Will asked, poking his head into her office.

"Come in," she said, motioning for him to have a seat. "I was just reflecting on the day."

"And?"

She smiled. "Overall, things went well."

"Overall?"

Her smile faded. She really needed to be careful about what she said to her brother. She didn't want to give him cause for worry where Jared was concerned. Not when there would never be anything between them anyway. "I had a patient leave before I finished."

He looked taken aback. "Someone left in the middle of your examination?"

"No," she clarified, shaking her head. "I stepped out to give a young girl a moment to think about getting a pelvic examination. When I came back to the room, she'd disappeared."

Will's confusion melted away to mild amusement. "I don't blame her. I'd run too if you tried to put me in stirrups."

Chelsea tossed her ink-pen cap at him. "You're not helping."

Grinning, he caught the plastic cap. "Apparently she wasn't ready for a pelvic. What's the problem?"

"She's sexually active. She came in to get a prescription for birth control. What if she ends up pregnant because she ran out instead of finishing her exam?"

"Then her pregnancy would be her fault. Not yours."

"But I should have—"

Will put up his hand. "Did you explain the reasons why she needed a pelvic exam?"

"Yes, but—"

"No buts. I'm sure you did a great job. The rest is up to the patient. You can't force people to make the right decisions for their health, Chels."

Talking to her brother could be like talking to a brick wall. Particularly as he was brilliant and usually made great sense.

"I know, but—"

"I already told you, no buts." Smirking, he winked. "Although I understand why you keep bringing mine up since it's so dashing."

"Your butt is dashing?" She gave a sisterly eye roll. "I swear I'd think you were insane if I didn't know how intelligent you really are."

"Thanks, sis." He leaned back, glanced around the office. His gaze lingered on the items she'd unpacked from her box, which included several photos of the two of them and friends. When his gaze returned to hers, his seriousness surprised her. "Was today everything you thought your first day would be?"

Not sure what had caused his mood to change, she nodded. "It was much more."

Because she'd seen Jared, touched Jared, refreshed her memory of just how powerfully he affected her mind and body. No, that was crazy. Jared was not why she was in Madison.

Will's brow lifted. "More?"

"Today wasn't much different than any other day for the past couple of years." After all, she'd been seeing patients for quite some time during her residency. "Yet because I was at a real job, with my own office and name tag..." she touched the gift he'd given her that morning "...today was magical."

Apparently pleased with her answer, Will nodded. "Good. You deserve magical. You ready to go out to celebrate?"

Chelsea glanced down at her spic-and-span desk. "I suppose. Is Jared going?"

She could have kicked herself for the slipup. No way should she be asking her brother about Jared. She'd always been subtle when she'd asked about him in the past, but there'd been nothing subtle about her blunt, heartfelt question just then.

"Said he was. Why?"

Under the intensity of her brother's stare, she fought the urge to blush. Something told her Will wouldn't be happy if she said that at seventeen she'd taken one look at Jared and had fallen for him hook, line, and sinker and today she'd discovered those feelings for him to be just as strong.

No matter how hard she tried, she couldn't keep her gaze locked on her brother's. "No reason other than I wondered who was going."

Her brother wasn't buying any of it. She didn't have to be looking into his eyes to know that.

"Sis." Will sounded resigned. "This isn't a good idea."

"What isn't a good idea?" She arched a brow and stared straight into his eyes.

"Jared."

"What about Jared?"

"I don't want you getting any ideas about him. He's not right for you." If it had been anyone other than Will talking she'd think they meant she wasn't good enough, but it was her brother. Will never thought any man was good enough for her. Certainly, he'd never liked Kevin.

"No worries, then, because my only interest in Jared is business." She hated lying, but she didn't want interference when there wasn't anything between her and Jared except memories of a passionate kiss and a brief heated look that morning that had quickly transformed into icicles.

"Just you make sure to keep it that way." Will's gaze flickered, causing suspicion to flare.

"Tell me something, Will. Why is it that I've not once seen Jared in the past ten years? Not even when I was interviewed for this job?"

"He was out of the country, doing mission work."

"I know he was on a mission trip and Jennifer wants to take off to go stay with her mother following her hip-replacement surgery, but don't you think it's a little odd that I've not seen Jared since that spring we all came down here?"

Will crossed his arms and took on a stubborn

look. "Not really, although I hadn't really thought about it. Is there any particular reason why you would have wanted to see him?"

Knowing she was revealing too much by questioning her brother, she shook her head. "No reason."

She got ready to leave for their dinner, but Will lingered.

"Look, sis, you should know that Jared…" He glanced around the room as if he'd find whatever word he searched for. "Well, he's got a bit of a reputation."

Ah, here came another brotherly warning. She'd known she'd said too much. "A reputation?"

"As a ladies' man."

She could remind her brother about his own reputation, but opted to hold her tongue, especially as she hadn't seen much to warrant that reputation since she'd moved to Madison. "And?"

"You shouldn't get any thoughts about him."

"Thoughts?" She blinked innocently, although she knew exactly what he meant.

"Non-professional ones, because in the long

run you'd end up getting hurt. He's never gotten over Laura."

Chelsea sighed with great exaggeration. "This is unnecessary, Will. I'm going to dinner with all the providers I work with, including you. Not on a date with Jared."

"Yes, but you're a beautiful woman and he's…" An irritated look came over his face.

"He's what?" she prompted, trying not to let her brother's offhand compliment sidetrack her from the real issue.

"Not blind," he ground out.

"Are you saying you think Jared might find me attractive?"

God, she hoped so. How pathetic was that when, even if he did, a relationship between them would never work?

"Not if he wants to live." Will smacked his fist into the palm of his other hand with emphasis.

Enough of the theatrics. She couldn't have her brother going all macho on his best friend. "Will," she said softly, "there's nothing for you to be concerned about."

"I'll be concerned when you're eighty when someone as jaded as Jared is involved."

She met her brother's stern expression and resisted the urge to hug him for loving her so much.

Will raked his fingers through his dark hair. "Don't get me wrong. He's my friend, a brilliant doctor, and we're lucky to have him, but he goes through women like a proctologist goes through rubber gloves."

"Eww." Chelsea scowled at her brother's analogy. "Bad comparison."

"But true." His jaw tightened. "Jared has only had one use for women since Laura died. I saw how you looked at him this morning, and I don't want to see you hurt, Chels."

He'd seen that look? No wonder he was issuing warnings.

"Will…" She sought the right words to tell her brother how much she loved and appreciated him, but wanted him to butt out when it came to her love life. Or lack of one, in this instance. "I'm twenty-eight years old and can decide for myself whether or not someone is worth the risk of getting hurt. Believe it or not, I'm not totally inexperienced," she said.

"Give me a name." Will's teeth gritted, his fists clenched at his sides, and she believed he really would go and fight for her honor.

Chelsea laughed. She couldn't help herself. Will's outrage was so adorable. "You can't go around bloodying every guy who finds me attractive."

"Wanna bet?"

She snickered in a very unlady-like way. "Lighten up. I'd like to marry and have kids someday."

Jared's babies. She closed her eyes and pictured blue-eyed, black-haired imps who called her mommy. Oh, what a fantasy.

"Just so long as you don't actually want Jared."

Had he read her mind?

"Even discounting the little-sister factor," he continued, "which is huge by the way, think how difficult a crash and burn between the two of you would make things at the office."

A nervous flutter gurgled in her belly, but she refused to acknowledge the warning. She gave him a smile meant to be light, but her attempt came out as forced. "I guess it's a good thing we're only going out for dinner as a group of coworkers, then."

"You're making fun of this, but I'm serious, Chels. Jared is a good guy, but Laura's death messed up his head. He's not been close to anyone since."

After ten years of carrying Jared in her heart and knowing she'd never have him, Will's warning fell flat.

Picking up her purse, she gave her brother a bright smile. "I'm going to dinner with my new coworkers. No big deal. Coming?"

After all, there was no reason for Will to get so worked up when, other than that brief moment this morning, Jared had looked as if he'd rather have his nails ripped off than have to spend five minutes in her company.

The recall of the cold look he'd given her earlier sent shivers racing down her spine. What had happened to cause his expression to go from burning hot to freezing cold?

Then she knew.

Will must have seen Jared's look, too, felt the sparks, and done what he'd just attempted to do with her.

Only Jared would have seen Will's warning as a sign that Chelsea was still interested in him, that she still wanted him.

He probably really was afraid she was going to corner him and jump his bones. Great.

No wonder he'd gone from hot to cold.

CHAPTER FOUR

AT THE restaurant, a cell phone buzzed and, after taking a call from the emergency room, Jennifer reluctantly excused herself from the group. Chelsea sat next to Will, opposite Jared, and Leslie between the two men.

She'd caught Jared looking at her several times while they'd waited for their table and after they'd been seated, but he always averted his gaze and distracted himself with conversation with Will.

Chelsea wanted to beat her head against the wall. Did he really think that after ten years she was going to doggedly pursue him? She'd barely pursued him after that wonderful week they'd met.

For ten years regrets had haunted her for

allowing Jared to push her away so easily. Of course, a few weeks later the girlfriend Chelsea hadn't known about had died. She'd tried contacting him, wanting him to know she felt his pain, that she would be there for him if he needed anything, that she'd turn eighteen in another week. She'd wanted him to know she missed him.

It had taken all her nerve to sneak into Will's things and find Jared's number, to dial it, and leave her message of condolence and ask him, please, to call her.

He hadn't called and that had spoken volumes. Heartbroken at yet again being rejected by someone whose love she'd craved, she'd resolved to focus on the things in her life that she had had control of. Like her medical career.

Besides, she was no longer a teenage girl with a crush. No, the heaviness clutching at her chest wasn't a teenage crush. But she daren't give a name to how Jared made her feel. How he'd always made her feel.

If whatever Will said to him was why he'd gone so cold on her she had to set the record straight, to let him know that she didn't expect anything more from him than friendship. Wanted, yes, expected, no.

After they placed their food order, she bit back the ball of nerves stifling her breath and locked gazes with him.

His blue eyes bore into hers with a ferocity that made her insides ache.

Which made her feel extremely self-conscious.

She held his gaze and reminded herself to be brave, to go after the personal life she wanted. Of course, she also wanted him to look at her and see beyond the flaws marring her body, to not care if she wore the badges of her parents' relentless efforts to make her into something she wasn't and never would be: perfect.

Too bad Cinderella's fairy godmother wasn't making house calls in Madison, Alabama.

Although her brother kept a watchful eye on her, he seemed distracted by the perky redhead to his left, who chatted a mile a minute about changes to the hospital's nursing staff.

If Jared was going to give her the cold shoulder, he had to stop looking at her with those hot eyes.

"Tell me how your first day went," Leslie said after the waiter served their drinks. She pushed a lock of her curly red hair away from her face.

Smiling at the woman she'd grown to like during her visits to Madison before coming to work at the clinic, Chelsea raved about her day, letting her real excitement overshadow all the doubts deep within her.

"You're going to live with Will for a while?"

"For now," she admitted. Will had insisted she stay with him, to give them time together. "I'll eventually look for a place of my own."

"There's no rush," Will interjected. "My place is big enough for us both."

His place was a gorgeous beach house that Chelsea had fallen in love with the first time she'd seen it several years back. Of course, she loved anything to do with the Gulf. Ever since the spring break she'd spent with Will and his friends in Gulf Shores, she'd adored the beach, felt energized when near the water.

"The view is spectacular," Leslie added, only to look away when Chelsea gave her a startled look. When had Leslie seen Will's view? She glanced back and forth between her brother and the nurse practitioner, searching for clues.

Leslie's quick smile and change of subject was clue enough.

"Jared, I've barely seen you since you got back from Guyana," she said, color high in her cheeks. "Tell me about your trip."

Jared traced his finger over the condensation forming on the outside of his glass. After a short hesitation he launched into tales of the people he'd met and treated during his six-week stint.

Having finished eating, Jared half listened to the conversation going on around him. Really, though, all his energy was focused on the woman sitting across from him. All evening he'd fought looking at her, fought the urge to find an excuse to touch her. God, she was beautiful. She'd taken her hair down from its ponytail at some point before they'd left the office. The dark, shiny strands teased her shoulders.

He'd like to run his fingers through her hair, to refresh his memory on just how soft her silky tresses were. Only he didn't recall wanting Chelsea this desperately all those years ago.

Yeah, he'd wanted her badly, enough that he'd made a horrible mistake, had hurt both Laura and Chelsea, but this burning inside him threatened to consume him.

His gaze met hers and his breath caught at the intensity with which she looked at him.

Great expectations shone in her sparkling eyes.

Which scared the hell out of him.

The only expectation he had in regard to Chelsea came with a hazardous-to-health warning.

Hadn't he learned his lesson? He couldn't have Chelsea. Not now, not ever. How could he do that to Laura's memory?

Very simply, he couldn't.

Not to mention the other hundred and one reasons why he had to throw barriers up between him and Chelsea. Things like her brother, the fact they worked together, the fact that although there were sparks between them he sensed just as much hesitation in her as he himself was experiencing. Perhaps more.

That hesitation intrigued him, made him want to peel away the layers covering who Chelsea really was.

But he wouldn't.

"I've got to run to the ladies' room," Leslie announced to no one in particular.

Jared didn't have a clue what had been said up to that point. All he'd noticed had been the dark desire in Chelsea's eyes, the tempting swell of her lips, the cautious tilt of her chin.

"Be back in a few." Will pushed his chair back and stood before Leslie had taken three steps away from the table.

Did they think they were fooling anyone? Perhaps he should give his friend a talk similar to the unnecessary one they'd had earlier in the day about Chelsea.

"Tonight has been fun. I'm glad you were able to make it after all." Although her voice remained upbeat, her eyes flashed with momentary uncertainty. The fact he found himself wanting to reassure her pushed him into doing the opposite.

"I really didn't have a whole lot of choice." He purposely roughened his voice. He couldn't deal with the awareness she caused. Not at the moment. Not when he was having to remind himself of his loyalty to Laura's memory. Not when he felt weak in the wake of Connie's bad news. He felt too raw inside. "As it was a business meal."

Chelsea picked up her napkin, folding it neatly at the crease. "We may not like the options, but there's always a choice."

"Your choice was to come to work in Madison?"

"To be near Will, yes."

"That's the only reason?"

"Not the only one." Her sultry eyes flashed with sweet meaning that was quickly masked, and he had to physically force himself not to take her hand in his. She didn't want him to see her attraction to him. Couldn't she feel the chemistry sparking between them?

Silence stretched, but he couldn't touch her comment, couldn't touch her.

"The Gulf," she added, taking a sip of water, clearing her throat when she drank too quickly. "Since that spring I first visited the Gulf, I've dreamed of living here."

"The hurricanes don't scare you?"

"Not enough to convince me to live some-where else." A slight tremble in her fingers, she set down her water glass. "What about you? The hurricanes bother you?"

"It's the winds no one knows are there until they drop down on you and rip everything in their path to shreds that bother me most."

"Did you have a lot of tornadoes in North Carolina?"

"Not many." He arched a brow that she knew

where he'd grown up and tried to recall just how much he'd told her that week when, as a teenager, she'd utterly fascinated him. To the point he'd forgotten she was his best friend's kid sister and that he had already committed to another.

When Chelsea's innocent lips had kissed him, he'd burst into flames, had forgotten she'd only been seventeen, a babe in many ways. Because in his arms she'd felt all woman and he'd wanted her more than any other woman, ever. Still did.

But that want had been wrong, had led him to another wrong, and in the end Laura had paid the ultimate price and he'd vowed to never make that mistake again.

Guilt hit him that he was sitting at a table with Chelsea, that he couldn't even look at her without wanting her, that even in a restaurant filled with a million smells, her sugar-cookie scent called to him.

Chelsea took a deep breath and even before she spoke warnings sounded in his head. "Have I done something to upset you?"

How the hell was he supposed to answer that?

"Because ten years is a long time to carry a grudge," she continued. "If you're worried I'm going to embarrass either of us by throwing myself at you again, don't be."

"This isn't necessary."

"Yes, it is. We work together, and it's clear you have issues with me working at the clinic. For everyone's sake, we need to at least be able to coexist."

She was right, of course. He'd known for months that his days of being able to avoid Chelsea had been coming to an end. That end was now here, and he was being forced to find a new way to deal with the guilt that seeing her gave him.

"We were once friends. I'd like us to be friends again, but perhaps only time will prove whether or not that's possible."

She wanted to be his friend? He couldn't do it. How could he ever justify that to Laura's memory?

"But if nothing else, we're going to have to at least develop a business relationship."

"Fine," he answered flippantly. "We'll have a business relationship, but make no mistake, Chelsea. There will never be anything more between us."

"I don't recall asking you for anything more," she reminded him in a soft but steady voice. "At least, not in this decade."

Wincing at his own stupid arrogance, Jared watched Chelsea abandon him to be the sole occupant of their table.

If he'd been Chelsea, he'd have walked away from his sorry butt, too.

The worst of it was, he didn't want her to walk away. Anything but.

CHAPTER FIVE

THE following morning Jared was dreading going into his next patient's exam room. Inside sat Connie Black, anxiously awaiting news on why her hip hurt so much. No doubt she expected him to tell her she had osteoarthritis or degenerative joint disease. Maybe even that she was going to need a hip replacement.

She wasn't expecting to learn that her cancer, the cancer she'd thought she'd beat, had metastasized to her left hip and destroyed the joint and surrounding bone tissue.

"You OK?" Leslie asked when she caught him lingering outside the doorway. She gave a concerned look and if he didn't get on the move she might ask what was wrong. Or she might ask more questions about last night's dinner because neither Will nor Leslie had bought his story about Chelsea needing some fresh air.

Memories of Chelsea's hurt expression caused Jared to momentarily question himself. A sense of foreboding hung over his head, like there was no escaping the emotional surge that went through him at just thinking of her. But he'd done the right thing to nip in the bud any thoughts she had about a relationship with him. If she disliked him, she wouldn't welcome his fascination for her. The fascination that had played out in vivid color during what little sleep he'd gotten the night before.

Regardless, he didn't want to go into the million and one things that had kept him awake most of the night.

He gave a quick nod of acknowledgement toward Leslie and knocked on the exam-room door. He'd procrastinated long enough and delaying the inevitable had never been his style.

He entered the exam room and instantly met Connie's pale blue eyes. When he'd first met her he'd thought her eyes similar to a Siberian husky's. Each time he saw her unusual eyes he was again struck by the image.

She sat in a chair against the wall opposite the exam table. The top of an elaborately carved dragonhead cane rested between her fingers. With all they'd been through the past few years, Connie was much more than a patient. More like a favorite aunt.

"So, what's the verdict, Dr Jared?" she asked, never one to beat about the bush. "Is this old hip going to get better any time soon?"

Jared pulled out the wheeled stool and, sliding the metal seat next to Connie, sat down. "I'm afraid not."

"That worn out, is it?" she asked, patting his hand. "Well, it's not like I expected to go jogging down the beach, anyway. Just so long as I can get to Monday night bingo, I'll get through. No worries."

Jared took her wrinkled hand and squeezed it, wishing he knew how to soften his words but knowing he had to give her the facts. "The MRI showed a tumor on your left hip, Connie. It's highly suspicious of cancer."

"Highly suspicious?" Her face paled, then hopeful Siberian blue eyes lifted. "If it's only suspicious, there's a chance it's not cancer?"

If only.

Jared flexed his jaw. He'd told patients in the past they had cancer without breaking down. For that matter, he'd told this woman. He could do it again. He steeled himself to do the job before him, strengthening his heart to carry on, all the while fighting the need to take Connie in his arms and just let her cry.

"I wish I could offer you hope, but I won't when I believe it would be false hope. I talked with the radiologist who read your MRI and, although he didn't say the actual words on your report, he's confident the tumor is a sarcoma."

Connie's lips disappeared into her mouth as emotion overtook her. Her shoulders slumped, and her eyes watered. "I can't go through this again, Dr Jared. I did once. I can't do it. Not again." She tugged on his hand. "Tell me this isn't happening."

Ignoring the tight squeezing in his chest, he held her watery gaze. "I spoke with a surgeon this morning and he reviewed your MRI films. He won't consider operating until you've had chemo to shrink the tumor."

Connie's free hand lifted to her salt-and-pepper hair. She'd lost all her hair during her previous cancer treatments.

"I'm not doing chemotherapy again." Shaking her head in denial, she twirled a short curl between her fingers as if she held something more precious than gold.

She did.

"I'm going to schedule an appointment with Dr Goodall—" he named her oncologist "—and let him review the MRI. He'll discuss your options, but with the way the hip joint has deteriorated, your prognosis doesn't look good."

"Why are you telling me this?"

Why indeed? Certainly not because he wanted to. There was nothing good about telling a woman cancer had taken hold so deeply her chance of survival wasn't good even with the recommended treatment. Without the chemotherapy she wouldn't survive more than a few months at most.

"I know you're upset, Connie," he began, wishing medical school had provided him with the right words to give comfort in times like these. Perhaps there were no words that comforted with dark diagnoses. Certainly he felt inadequate to the task. "But you're a strong woman and you will beat this."

She had to.

"I've already beaten it." Connie's words came out in a high pitch. "At least, I thought I had. Really, I was just fooling myself."

Jared's stethoscope weighed heavily around his neck, threatening to choke him. "You did beat your lung cancer. This is a new battle, but one you'll also win."

"You don't really believe that, do you, Dr Jared?" Her intelligent gaze sought his, pinned him beneath her intent stare.

What could he say? At best, the cancer would be localized to her hip and, after eradication of the tumor, she'd need total hip replacement and months and months of rehabilitation. At worst, the PET scan he'd order would reveal metastasized cancer in other areas of her body. If that was the case, modern medicine would be able to do very little to preserve Connie's life.

Connie remaining positive, believing in her chances of survival, would be the vital key to her overcoming her cancer. If he took all hope away from her he may as well shut the lid on her coffin and nail it closed.

Hope always existed. Miracles happened every day, and Connie was due a miracle.

"You will get through this."

"If only Paul were here…" Her voice trailed off and she sighed.

"He's watching over you, Connie. You know he is."

Lowering her head, the woman nodded. "I miss him."

Pain at Connie's loss pricked Jared's heart. If

ever love existed, Connie and Paul Black had shared the elusive emotion.

"I know you do," he said softly. He himself missed the man's positive outlook and robust laughter. He could only imagine Connie's loneliness and sense of loss.

Her hand trembled within his grasp. "Maybe this is the Lord's way of bringing us back together."

"No!"

Connie jerked back.

Jared hadn't meant his outburst to startle her. Hell, his shout had startled him. He lifted Connie's hand, holding the fragile fingers with care. "You have to fight. Paul would want you to beat this. For your daughter. Your grandsons."

She patted his cheek with her free hand, then leaned her head against his shoulder and cried. Feeling awkward, Jared let her.

Although the delay put him behind with his other patients, he spent another thirty minutes with Connie, scheduling her PET scan to see if there were any other hot spots in her body. He prayed the scan would reveal only the tumor in her hip. Fortunately, she'd had a negative PET scan a little more than a year before as part of her routine cancer follow-up. Perhaps the disease really hadn't metastasized outside the hip joint.

He'd hope for the best.

He moved through the rest of the day in a daze, seeing his patients but unable to focus on anything other than the defeated look on Connie's face when she'd left the office.

In the past twenty-four hours he'd hurt two women who elicited powerful emotions inside him.

With Connie, he'd had no choice. And with Chelsea, well, there really hadn't been a choice there either.

He glimpsed her from time to time in the hallway. Although he'd felt her gaze on him, he'd carefully avoided looking at her. Each time he thought of her hurt look the night before, he pushed his guilt aside, letting the fresh keep company with the old. Guilt was something he had an overabundance of.

* * *

Two weeks later, frustration plagued Chelsea. Despite their working similar schedules, Jared managed to ignore her almost completely. Oh, there were the occasional glances when he thought she wasn't looking, but the moment their eyes met he'd get busy or disappear.

At times his rejection felt like salt poured into the wounds of her childhood. Into the wounds of his rejection when she'd been seventeen. She still wasn't good enough.

Perhaps that was for the best because there was no place for a relationship between her and Jared to go, and she'd only end up hurting even more.

"Hey, sis." Will popped into her office and caught her daydreaming. "Why the long face?"

"No long face." She immediately stretched said long face into a smile. "Just thinking."

"About?" He plunked himself down in the chair across from her desk.

"Your birthday," she covered. Actually, she and Leslie had discussed his birthday earlier. They'd decided to throw a party. "This is the first year in some time that we'll be together. What are your plans for the big day?"

He shrugged. "Just another day in my book."

"Another day?" This coming from the man who'd always made a big deal of her birthday? Perhaps he'd been trying to make up for their parents who'd repeatedly failed to acknowledge the day as anything out of the ordinary. Even while she'd been away at medical school, Will had always found a way to make her day special. "Ha, don't try to fool me. You live for birthdays."

He gave a disheartened sigh. "That was before I was turning thirty-five."

"Thirty-five on a man looks good."

"There is that." He grinned devilishly.

"So, can I take you out for the big night, or do you have other plans you wouldn't want a little sister tagging along on?"

"As you live with me, you know what a dull life I lead. I'm free."

"Why is that?" Surprisingly, Will went out in the evenings less than she would have thought.

Not that working the hours he did was dull. Just that he'd always been a social bug and now, well, he wasn't. She'd come to Madison expecting to spend a lot of evenings home alone. Instead, with the exception of the nights he worked in the emergency room, Will almost always kept her company.

Not that she minded. Spending time with her brother had always been one of her favorite things.

"Parties and such don't hold as much appeal as they once did." Her brother sounded like he was ready to settle down. If only she knew a nice girl to introduce him to. Unfortunately she hadn't done much socializing since moving to Madison. Other than the girls at the office, she didn't know anyone.

Then again, she had picked up on vibes between Will and Leslie every time the two had been within ten feet of each other. Although, honestly, she wondered if they weren't avoiding each other, the way Jared was ignoring her.

Did Will even know Leslie was attracted to

him? Maybe not because men could be so blind at times. She smiled, thinking Will's party would be the perfect time to help him see the jewel under his nose.

"I hear you." She was agreeing with his comment about parties, while in her mind she continued to plot on what a fabulous event his party would be. The grandest birthday ever. Will deserved that and more.

"When were you a party animal?" He had the audacity to laugh. "All I recall is a little girl too determined to prove her parents wrong for her to ever actually have any fun."

Ouch. She had been too busy studying to party.

"I have fun." Not recently, but who was counting? "And our parents have nothing to do with why I became a doctor."

"Don't they?" Will's question was low.

Did he think she'd spent all those years training for a profession she didn't love?

"If anything, Mum and Dad should have turned me off medicine. I'm here because it's where I want to be. I love taking care of people."

Will sat silent for a few minutes. "I talked to Jared," her brother commented dryly.

She met his gaze, trying to keep her interest to a normal level. "About?"

"Just wanted to make sure the record was clear."

"On?" she asked, although she had a horrible suspicion she knew exactly to what he referred.

"You."

"A total waste of your time, but if it makes you feel better." She waved her hand dismissively, picking up a lab report off her desk and pretending to study it.

"It does."

"Fine. Makes no difference to me." Liar, liar, pants on fire. She initialed the lab report, indicating she'd seen the results, then placed the paper in her out basket.

She busied herself with shuffling through the mail, trashing numerous pharmaceutical advertisements without bothering to open the brightly packaged envelopes, anything to keep from having to meet her brother's intense gaze.

"Right." He got up and headed toward the door.

"Wait! What did he say?" She shouldn't ask, but when it came to Jared she didn't seem capable of resisting.

Will paused, turned, met her eyes with mischievous brown ones. He'd set her up. Given her slack on the line, then hooked her good. "I can't recall. Good thing it makes no difference, eh?"

Brothers!

"Tell me."

Will's eyes narrowed, and he crossed his arms. "I suggested he bring a date to the surprise party you'll inevitably throw for my birthday."

"A date?" she choked out, ignoring that he'd guessed what she had planned for his big day. The smug fink.

"As in someone other than you because you, my dear sister, are off-limits."

Jared skimmed over the faxed consultation letter from Dr Goodall. The specialist had seen

Connie Black in a follow-up of her PET scan yesterday. Connie's cancer wasn't confined to her hip joint. The disease had invaded her liver, pancreas, and colon. She was scheduled for chemotherapy in three weeks. Dr Goodall recommended immediate therapy but according to his letter, Connie had asked for the extra time before starting treatment.

He wished she hadn't delayed, but thank God she'd agreed to undergo chemotherapy again. The harsh medicines were her only hope of surviving her cancer.

Over the years he'd been practicing medicine, he'd lost numerous patients. All doctors did. But Connie was different. The feisty older woman touched his heart deeply, and he'd foregone all professional detachment where she was concerned.

Perhaps it was because she'd taken everything life had dished out in her stride. At least, she had until Paul had died. Her husband had been her rock and had stood by her side throughout her struggles. Other than his parents, Jared had never known two people to be closer, so connected.

He and Laura had shared friendship, had grown up together, and had always thought they'd spend their lives together. But if he was honest with himself, he'd admit that although he and Laura had shared a connection, it hadn't been of the same intensity that the Blacks had shared, that his parents shared.

He stood, raked his fingers through his hair. God, it had been a long day. He was ready to work out his frustrations at the gym.

Speaking of connections, the moment he stepped into the hallway he bumped into Chelsea, a pretty breath of fresh air who was also calling an end to her day. No matter how many times he ordered his eyes elsewhere, he drank in the sight of her trim figure.

She wore dark slacks, a soft chenille blouse, and a nervous smile.

Why had he had to bump into her tonight? When he felt vulnerable. When he was thinking about couples like his parents and the Blacks. Couples who embodied something real.

He'd wanted that once upon a time. A connection that would last a lifetime. Beyond a lifetime.

He met Chelsea's warm brown eyes and saw everything he'd ever wanted but had quit believing in.

Something he didn't deserve.

Not after what he'd done to Laura.

He couldn't—shouldn't—want Chelsea, and he couldn't believe. Not in her. She was Will's sister and his coworker. Totally off-limits in the only way he allowed himself to get close to a woman.

Sure, he was attracted to her, always had been, but that didn't mean he had to have her.

"Jared." She moistened her lower lip and the sight of her pink tongue punched him in the gut, flooded him with memories. She hesitated, but only for a moment. "Do you have a minute?"

"If this is about the other night…" he began. He'd said everything that warranted saying.

Nothing had changed. Chelsea deserved better than anything he could ever give her and he wouldn't risk his friendship with Will, risk a career he enjoyed, for a quickie with a coworker.

A quickie with Chelsea would never be enough, anyway. From the beginning he'd wanted more than that from her, which was what had led to the domino effect straight to hell.

"It's not," she quickly denied. "You made yourself clear. You aren't interested in me." She took a deep, heart-tugging breath. "I accepted that a long time before I came to Madison."

She had?

That was quick. Easy. Too easy. Which irked. Irked even more that he cared it irked. He didn't care. He didn't.

She toyed with the zipper on her purse. "This is about my brother."

"Will?"

"I only have one. Thank God."

But the way she said the words made him think Chelsea would have welcomed a dozen such brothers. Jared wouldn't know. His mother had had problems with his delivery and never conceived again. Having a brother like Will would have been fun. Certainly, they'd had a good time in med school. Will had been his best friend for over ten years, had seen him through the hell with Laura.

"I'm throwing a surprise birthday party for him."

Surprise? Should he tell her Will knew about the party?

"Maybe not so surprise. I know he knows." She gave a sheepish look and sighed. "He told me he asked you to bring a date."

"He specifically requested my date not be you," he told her just in case there was any doubt in her mind about where her brother's intentions had been. Will knew his history, and he couldn't blame his friend for wanting him to stay away from his sister. If he'd had a sister, he wouldn't want her with a man like him either. Not after Laura and how he'd broken her heart, basically killed her.

"He told me that, too." She curved her full lips into a smile that didn't quite reach her eyes, hinting that she forced her pleasantness. "I was hoping I could ask a favor."

"A favor?"

Standing across from him, she looked calm, but the heightened color in her cheeks told another story.

"I love my brother very much." She toyed with the zipper again. "With medical school, I haven't been able to spend as much time with him as I would have liked over the past few years. In the process I hadn't realized how cut off he was."

"Cut off?" Jared wasn't sure he was following her train of thought.

"Socially."

He didn't like where this particular train was headed.

"Uh-uh. I don't like where you're going with this and will have no part in it."

She frowned. "But you've not heard what I wanted to say."

"I don't need to. You want me to set Will up with a date."

"Yes. Sort of." She sounded surprised. Did

she think he couldn't see the thoughts so plainly broadcast in those gorgeous eyes?

"Will's a big boy. If he wants a date, he'll bring his own."

Chelsea scowled. "Tell me, was my brother dating before I arrived in Madison? Is it my fault he's home every night?"

Jared thought back, pulling forward a few faces, although none in recent months. But Jared didn't keep tabs on Will's social life. Besides, Will never seemed to stick with the same woman long. Jared understood that.

"He dated."

Chelsea didn't look impressed. "Uh-uh. When?"

Jared scowled. "What do I look like? His social secretary?"

Chelsea's eyes pinned him where he stood. "So you don't really know if he was dating or not? Is that what you're saying?"

"No, I don't." But he did know he didn't like the current conversation.

A worried look played on her face. "I don't

think he was. I think he's either ready to fall in love or already has."

Maybe he should be grateful he'd been an only child.

"You're insane."

"You're just now figuring that out?" Her plump lips twitched. "Most people notice that about me right away."

He shook his head at how easily she joked about herself. But something in her voice told a bigger story, hinting at hurt beneath the flippant façade. Hinting that perhaps she believed things she shouldn't.

"Look." He started over, wondering why he wanted to peel away the layers and see the real Chelsea. Why he cared if her pretty smile hid a great deal of pain. Why she made him so nervous. "Your brother is a grown man and more than capable of knowing what he wants and doesn't want. If he's met someone, that's his business. You should stay out of his affairs."

Her smile fading, Chelsea crossed her arms and glared at him. "My brother is my business."

"Like warning me off from you was his business?"

Her gaze narrowed, and he could tell he'd caught her off guard, that he'd made her stop and think about what she'd said. Will should appreciate his efforts.

"He shouldn't have done that because there's nothing between us." She was lying and they both knew it. Whether either of them welcomed the heat, sparks exploded whenever they were near. "Besides," she continued, "that's different."

"Different?" He almost laughed at the stubborn expression on her face. Maybe he would have had it been anyone but Chelsea. "Why?"

"Because…" She paused, the skin around her clenched knuckles whitened. She didn't finish but not because she didn't know how to answer.

"Look." She straightened her fingers and smoothed her slacks. "I don't want to argue. I just wondered if you thought there was something between Will and Leslie."

"Hold up." Jared put his hands in the air to halt

her. "You think Will and Leslie…no way. They work together and know better than to do something so stupid." Sure, he suspected something had happened between his two friends, but they'd obviously seen reason and called whatever it had been to an end.

Was she wanting Will to have an office romance so she could prove some point about an office romance working?

Sure, he'd admit it might for a short time, but an office romance was nothing more than a recipe for disaster. Even if all the other barriers between him and Chelsea didn't exist, he still wouldn't touch her. Not with them working in the same office.

"Have you thought about going to work somewhere else?"

Where the hell had that come from? Surely not his mouth.

But the crazy question had.

Chelsea's eyes widened with surprise, then she narrowed her eyes at him, but he refused to squirm.

"If I didn't know better," she said, "I'd think you didn't like me, Jared."

"I don't."

For a moment her golden eyes darkened and he regretted his quick denial. After all, as much as he wanted to not like her, he couldn't help but do so. Even with avoiding her as much as possible, he wasn't blind. The clinic was a brighter place since she'd arrived. Like the idiot he was, he wanted a closer inspection of the light shining within her, even if that closer inspection zapped the life out of him.

"Yes, you've made your feelings about me abundantly clear," she ground out, failing to hide her hurt.

Why had he asked such a stupid question? Because it irked that she'd acted as if she no longer wanted him? Idiot. Wasn't that what he wanted? Will was a safe topic. One that constantly reminded him he'd been threatened if he so much as looked twice at Chelsea. Admittedly, had his own reasons, his own guilt, not checked his desire, nothing would have kept him from pursuing her.

"Chelsea, I…" He stopped, unsure how to go on. To say anything more would be wrong. The past wasn't going to go away. He wasn't going to change his mind and she wasn't going to change jobs. Even if she did by some miracle go to work elsewhere, he still wouldn't become involved with her.

Since Laura, he didn't do involvement. Ever. Short, physically driven relationships, yes. Involvement, never. No matter where Chelsea worked, she was Will's baby sister and Will was his business partner and best friend. A lethal combination.

Her gaze searched his, hopeful, and despite her earlier words, he knew interest still flared. She hadn't gotten over him, not by a long shot.

And although a selfish, very male part of him felt joyous that her interest hadn't waned, another part felt like a heel. Chelsea was a beautiful, intelligent woman who deserved better. He understood why Will wanted him to bring a date.

Will wanted his sister to move on, to find

someone who would never treat her the way he'd treated Laura.

Although Chelsea's interest flattered the hell out of him and made keeping things strictly business all the more difficult, Jared understood his partner's feelings.

For his and Chelsea's sakes, he'd do his part to oblige.

CHAPTER SIX

LATER that week, Betty stopped Chelsea just before she saw her next patient. "Will's been called to the emergency room," the nurse said.

"He's asked for his patients to be split between you, Dr Jared, and Leslie so one of you won't get stuck working late, trying to see them all. Only Leslie isn't feeling well, and I hate to add to her load." Betty gave a concerned tongue click. "Is it OK if Kayla and I divvy up his patients between you and Dr Jared instead?"

"I don't think that'll be a problem. At least, not on my part." She actually looked forward to being busy as the extra patients would help keep her mind off Jared. More and more he haunted her dreams, day and night. "You might ask

Jared just to make sure he doesn't mind, though."

"Will do."

She stopped the nurse from leaving. "Is Leslie OK?"

"Just a stomach bug," Betty assured her. "Goodness knows, we've seen enough of them lately it's a wonder we all aren't heaving."

"Leslie's throwing up?"

The petite redhead and Chelsea had gone to lunch together a few times. The more Chelsea got to know the nurse practitioner, the more she liked her and the more she knew Leslie was the perfect woman for her brother. She hated the thought of her not feeling well.

"Poor thing," she commiserated. "Maybe she should go home."

Chelsea would call Will and have him stop by to check on Leslie before coming home. Maybe the two could work through whatever was keeping them apart. Although her brother refused to talk about Leslie, Chelsea knew something was between them. And that something had driven them apart. She just hoped that something wasn't her arrival.

"She won't go." Betty shook her head in a motherly fashion, despite the fact she had to be close to Chelsea's and Leslie's age. "She says the clinic is too busy for her to go lie around when she feels fine except for the nausea."

Chelsea admired Leslie's dedication and recalled many a time as a resident of working through whatever illness she'd happened to pick up from constant exposure.

"If she needs help with her afternoon patient load, be sure to let me know. I'll help any way I can and don't mind staying late if needed."

Betty nodded. "Just taking some of Dr Will's patients will be enough, but I'll tell her if she needs help to give you a holler."

Chelsea entered the patient room and was surprised to see Hannah Belew sitting on the exam table. Betty must have been distracted by Leslie's illness and Will being called to the emergency room or else she'd have forewarned her that the runaway patient had returned.

"I'm back," the teenager announced, giving her a sheepish look. Hannah wore her hair pulled away from her face, revealing a tiny silver hoop through her left eyebrow that Chelsea didn't think had been there during her last visit.

"I see that." She acknowledged the girl's presence, washed her hands, and sat on the stool. She didn't want to blow this second chance to reach Hannah, not when she might possibly make a difference in her life. "What can I do for you today?"

"Not a pelvic," the girl said quickly.

"That's always your choice."

"But…" her mouth twisted in thought "…I read the brochure you gave me, and I think I should get the vaccine."

"The vaccine for HPV?"

"That's the one. Can I take it in my arm or do I have to take it in my butt?"

"Hip," Chelsea replied automatically.

"Hip, butt, same difference."

Chelsea smiled. The fact Hannah had come

back meant the first visit hadn't been a total loss. Which meant she might have done something right.

"I want the shot." Hannah pushed an escaped strand of dark hair away from her face. "My mom checked with our insurance and our plan covers immunizations."

"You talked with your mom about this?" Chelsea was impressed.

"Well, it's not like getting the shot means I'm sexually active since it's recommended to have it before you have sex." Hannah pointed out, clueing Chelsea in on what had been discussed and what hadn't.

"Yes," she agreed. "The idea behind the vaccine is to provide immunity prior to exposure."

"I told my mom about the vaccine, and she agrees I should get it. She may bring my little sister in soon to discuss the vaccine, too."

Chelsea entered the order for the immunization into the electronic chart, then gave a friendly smile. "Hannah, are you still with your boyfriend?"

"Yes."

Which meant she was still sexually active.

"But you're not interested in a pelvic exam?" she asked, just to make sure, to give Hannah the opportunity to change her mind or to ask questions.

"No." The girl hesitated then continued. "But I am making Brett use condoms. I figure there isn't a reason for me to go on the Pill, which means I don't need a Pap smear or whatever it is you said I'd get."

"A thin prep. It's a liquid-based test for cervical abnormalities, including HPV," Chelsea reminded her, pleased with Hannah's choice to protect herself. "Condoms aren't foolproof, but you're wise to make him wear one because it does cut down on your risk of possible exposure."

"He was a virgin, too, you know." Hannah's voice took on a defensive edge. "It's not like he can give me anything."

"Not as long as you remain his only partner."

Hannah's gaze narrowed, and she stared at

Chelsea with distrust. "You sound like you think he'll cheat and give me some disease."

"I hope he doesn't, but if he did it wouldn't be the first time something like that's happened to a young girl. Actually, that scenario happens to women of all ages."

Hannah considered her for a long time, then asked, "Did it happen to you?"

"No." Chelsea shook her head. Kevin hadn't cheated on her—that she knew of anyway. Perhaps it would have been easier if he had. Instead he'd drifted out of her life following the revelation of her back. She should have known better than to let him see the real her. Her own parents hadn't been able to love her—why had she thought Kevin could? "But a woman is better to be safe than sorry. Taking responsibility for your health isn't always easy or pleasant. But if you aren't willing to take on that responsibility, who is, right?"

"True," the girl conceded. She fidgeted on the table, hinting she wanted to say more. "Brett doesn't like condoms, but he wears one. At first he thought I didn't trust him. But other than to tell me the barrier cuts down on what he feels, he hasn't complained since I explained I had to get a pelvic exam to go on the Pill. He doesn't want me to have to do anything that would hurt me." She shot Chelsea a look. "Even if it means he enjoys sex less."

Chelsea heard the unspoken implication "because he loves me". Perhaps Brett did.

"They make special types of condom that won't desensitize him so much." Chelsea suggested a few brands. "They can be a little more expensive, but it'll feel more natural."

Hannah nodded.

"The important thing is that you always use a condom if you're going to remain sexually active."

"Yeah, that's what I told Brett. He says he'll protect me however he can." The young girl's dreamy-eyed smile both touched Chelsea and worried her. She only hoped the boy deserved Hannah's adoration and never hurt her.

She spent a few more minutes talking with

Hannah, answering questions about the vaccine and when she'd need to return for the second shot in the series of three.

Chelsea's next patient presented with vague symptoms. Fatigue. Generalized muscle aches. Just not feeling quite like herself. Tammy Jones denied any other symptoms and Chelsea ordered tests. When she'd finished, she stepped out and bumped into Betty.

"Oh, I was just coming to find you. Lacey Donaldson is in room four. Her family made her come. She's seen Dr Jared or Will in the past, but Dr Jared is tied up suturing a fifty-six-year old woman who fell at the grocery store and gashed her arm. Lacey's mother is afraid Lacey will leave if she has to wait."

"Lacey Donaldson?" The name sounded familiar.

"Her son is in Madison Memorial's pediatric wing. Today is the first day Lacey's left the hospital since her car wreck."

"Oh." The name clicked in Chelsea's mind. "Will mentioned Caden Donaldson."

He'd told her about the four-year-old who'd been unrestrained in a motor vehicle accident. The young boy had taken a hard blow to the head that had left him in a coma. That had been last week.

"Has Caden regained consciousness?"

"No, he's being kept sedated to cut down on brain damage until the swelling begins to subside."

Poor little boy. And poor mother. Chelsea could hardly imagine the emotional ordeal the woman was going through.

"Is Lacey sick, or is the stress getting to her?"

"The stress. She looks awful, bless her heart." Betty sighed. "Georgia made her go home to shower, change clothes, and get some of her things to have at the hospital."

"Lacey's a single mom?" She recalled Will mentioning the girl only had her mother for support. Tragic really.

Betty nodded. "She tries real hard, works two jobs and goes to night school. This has devastated her."

"Thanks for letting me know she's here." Chelsea entered the room, but wasn't prepared for the sad barely out-of-her-teens girl sitting on the exam table. Lacey Donaldson had been a beautiful girl once upon a time, but she looked like someone had poked a straw into her and sucked out every drop of life. Dark circles rimmed her sunken eyes. Chalky white best described her skin pallor. She'd pulled her hair back in a tight ponytail. Overall, she looked gaunt and frail.

A worried-looking fifty-ish woman sat in the extra chair present in the exam room. Her hands folded in her lap, she sadly watched her daughter's every move.

"Hi, Lacey. I'm Dr Chelsea Majors. Dr Will Majors is my brother. I've been at the clinic for a few weeks," she said, hoping to make the young woman feel more at ease with her. "Dr Jared is in with an emergency, so I'll be examining you."

"I don't need to be here," Lacey informed her with an upset glance at her mother.

"You've barely eaten or slept for two weeks," the older woman scolded. "Of course you need to be here."

The girl's eyes turned imploring. "How could I eat when Caden just lies there? Having to be fed through a tube? I don't want to eat anything and when I try I want to throw up."

Chelsea sat down on her stool and met the young woman's hollow gaze. "Your son needs you to take care of yourself. If you let yourself get run-down, and, honestly, I think you already have, Caden isn't going to understand why you're sick and unable to tend to him when he wakes up."

"You don't understand."

"As someone who has dealt with other patients with family members who pushed themselves too hard and got sick, I do know what you're doing isn't good for you or Caden," she said gently. "He needs you healthy."

"She's not slept more than a few hours since the crash," Georgia added, giving her daughter a stern but love-filled look. "She's recovering from her own injuries. I've tried to get her to go home for a good night's sleep, told her I'd stay with Caden, but she won't leave his bedside."

"What if he wakes up and I'm not there?" The young mother's face pinched painfully. "What if he wakes up right now and wants his mommy, and I'm not there? I should never have left." Tears in her eyes, she glanced accusingly at Georgia. "You shouldn't have made me leave my baby."

"Not eating. Not sleeping. Living on adrenaline and fear." Georgia tsked with eyes full of compassion. "Lacey, I love my grandson, but I'm just as worried about you. No matter how old you are, you're my baby girl, and I hate to see you doing this to yourself."

"Don't worry about me." Lacey sounded angry. No doubt she was angry at the world and would inadvertently take out her frustrations on her mother. "Worry about my precious little boy lying in that hospital bed, fighting for his life," she demanded.

"Lacey." Chelsea brought the young

woman's attention back to her because Georgia looked on the verge of tears. Although it was natural for Lacey to lash out, that didn't mean her words didn't wound those she inflicted them on. "Making yourself ill isn't helping Caden or yourself."

"I'm not ill," she insisted, looking ready to storm out of the exam room. Fatigue washed over her tiny frame and her shoulders sagged. "I'm sorry. I know I'm not thinking clearly, but what would you have me do? Go on with my life and pretend my precious baby isn't lying in that hospital bed, dying?"

Chelsea's heart squeezed.

"No, I wouldn't have you pretend anything. Neither do I want you to assume Caden isn't going to pull through this. You have to remain positive."

"Positive?" Lacey screeched. "Do you know that Dr Westland told me if Caden survives he'll likely have brain damage? That he might be mentally retarded or blind or paralyzed or…"

Lacey's voice choked and she burst into tears.

Georgia went to her daughter, embracing her in a hug. Lacey shook her hand, waving her mother away.

"No. I won't have your sympathy for me. Not when I did this to him." Her eyes hollow orbs, she turned to Chelsea. "I was the one who caused the crash that did this to Caden. I wasn't paying attention that he'd undone his safety-belt catch on his car seat. It's my fault he's like this."

The woman's pain echoed through the room, instilling itself into Chelsea's heart.

"You didn't crash your car on purpose."

"No, that car pulled out in front of me and I swerved to miss it and lost control." Lacey closed her eyes, shuddering with memories. "We flipped and flipped. I can't remember how many times. The car just kept rolling."

"What happened to Caden was an accident."

"If he'd had his seat belt on he might not have been hurt. I should have known he'd taken it off."

Chelsea and Georgia both started speaking, but Lacey shook her head.

"Don't deny it. I heard the police officer say that if Caden had been restrained, he probably wouldn't have been hurt. He's right. Look at me." Lacey held out her scraped arms. "I barely have a scratch, and my baby is lying in that hospital bed not able to breathe for himself."

"There are a lot of things in life difficult to understand. How one person is born healthy, another not. Why accidents happen to some people, yet others are constantly careless and remain unscathed. Each of us has to make the best of what we're given, Lacey." About these things Chelsea knew a lot. Many a night as a little girl she'd cried herself to sleep wondering why her, why her back that was so crooked and malformed, why her parents who insisted on surgery after surgery in search of perfection. "Whatever happens with Caden," she softly assured her, "he'll still be your little boy, and you'll still love him."

Lacey stared blankly ahead.

"You need to eat. I'm going to ask your mother to make sure you have access to at least one healthy meal a day. Preferably two." Chelsea glanced at Georgia, who promptly nodded her agreement. "I need you to promise you'll do your best to eat what she brings you."

Lacey closed her eyes, her expression pained. "I'll try."

"Good," Chelsea said. "And sleep? Will you try that, too?"

"I can't sleep," Lacey protested, looking agitated again. "When I close my eyes, my brain won't shut off to let me. All I see when I shut my eyes is the same thing I see when I open them. A nightmare. A horrible, horrible nightmare that won't go away. My Caden unconscious and just lying there, not moving or talking or even knowing I'm there."

Sobs racked Lacey's frail body. Although the woman's frustrations and pain were all too real and understandable, her lack of sleep and nutrition left her even less capable of coping.

"I'd like to give you a mild sedative for you to take before trying to rest. It's mild enough that when Caden wakes up, you'll rouse without problems," Chelsea said, knowing the woman wouldn't take anything that would keep her away from her son. "But it's strong enough that you should be able to sleep."

Eyes wide, Lacey shook her head. "I don't want to take drugs."

"This would only be short-term. Just something to take the edge off so you can rest. Sleep really is important, Lacey. Without sleep you aren't going to be able to think clearly. Dr Westland might need your input regarding Caden's care. If he does, you need your mind sharp so you can make good decisions. You said yourself that you weren't thinking clearly," she gently pointed out. "Fatigue can make your mind cloudy, and it's easy to make poor choices when you're exhausted. If for no other reason, rest for Caden's sake."

Tears still streaming down her cheeks, Lacey regarded her for a few minutes. "OK. I'll take them. I don't like the idea of taking medicines, but I like the thought of making a bad decision about Caden even less."

Chelsea spoke with the young woman several more minutes, explaining how the medicine worked and when it was and wasn't appropriate to take it.

After Georgia and Lacey had left, Chelsea remained in the exam room feeling emotionally exhausted, feeling vulnerable. She wasn't ready to face her next patient. Not yet. Not without a minute or two to process the emotions running through her at Lacey's pain and guilt. The woman needed counseling. Lots of counseling. But to have suggested counseling now would have meant pulling Lacey away from Caden's bedside, and she would never agree. Not at this point.

Chelsea leaned her head against the wall, taking a moment to pull herself together.

She really couldn't imagine the heartache and guilt Lacey was going through. Neither did she know if she'd said the right things, if she'd given her enough help. She'd check into what resources and support groups were available through Madison Memorial Hospital. Maybe there was a social worker who could get Lacey help while Caden recovered.

How would Lacey cope if the little boy didn't pull through?

Chelsea shuddered at the thought of what might happen. No, she wouldn't think of that. But she would make a point of ensuring Lacey had access to a crisis hotline and a good social worker, just in case.

She closed her eyes and said a quick prayer that Caden would fully recover.

"You OK?"

Chelsea looked up into concerned blue eyes that held the power to heal the ache in her heart and answer a lifetime of prayers. They also held the power to hurt her as no one else could.

"Jared."

He placed his hand on her shoulder. Warmth and need spread through her.

Without thought she wrapped her arms around him, needing the comfort of feeling close to another person. To him.

* * *

Jared's entire body stiffened, but he couldn't bring himself to pull away from Chelsea. His arms slipped around her waist, holding her, yet he didn't allow himself to relax into the embrace.

She looked so shaken. After three weeks of seeing her in action, he knew she was a great doctor but didn't maintain professional detachment.

He felt completely unable to suggest she armor her heart. Not when, no matter how much he desired an impenetrable shield of professional detachment himself, he hadn't figured out a way to armor his own heart. His involvement with Connie Black proved that. Lacey, too.

Hell, professional detachment was something even the most highly skilled and experienced of providers struggled with from time to time. The very essence of a person that led them into the medical field made them more susceptible to others' needs, others' emotions.

Speaking of Chelsea's heart, he could feel her heartbeat against his chest, could feel her heat seeping through his clothes as she snuggled against him. His arms dropped, hanging at his sides, feeling like heavy tree trunks because he should push her away yet couldn't.

Neither holding her nor pushing her away felt right, so he just stood there.

Who was he kidding? This caring woman against him felt right. Too right. Just as she had when she'd barely been seventeen and had kissed him, she made him want things he had no business wanting.

Which was as wrong now as wanting her had been then, just for different reasons.

So he let her lean on him, feeling awkward and totally removed from himself, because if he let the fact Chelsea pressed against him register completely, he'd be a goner.

Seeming to realize what she was doing, she pulled back and shot him an apologetic glance.

"Sorry," she mumbled in a low voice, her cheeks rosy.

By not responding, he'd embarrassed her, which he'd never intended. He'd taken one look at her

ashen face and had had to let her know he understood, had wanted to ease the burden on her heart.
Instead, he'd set himself up to hurt her yet again.

Despite never wanting to hurt this woman, he
seemed to be capable of nothing else. But, then,
wasn't that what he did? Hurt the women he got
close to? And wouldn't it have been much worse
to hold her close when doing so would only
leave them both wanting more?

He already wanted more. Lots more.

If they became involved, he may as well kiss
his life in Madison goodbye.

He wouldn't risk it. Not even for someone
whose scent haunted his senses long into the
night and had from the day he'd met her. Even
if he'd been in denial of that fact for years. Now
that he'd held her again, heaven help him, he'd
feel the heat of her body in his dreams.

Still, he couldn't stand seeing her hurt. After
all, even if they could never have a personal relationship, they did work together. Coworkers
could commiserate over a particularly tough
patient.

"I came as soon as Betty told me Lacey was here. You've seen her already?" he asked.

"She and her mother just left." Not meeting his eyes, Chelsea nodded. "I guess you think I'm silly for being so upset over a woman I've never met before today."

"No," he answered honestly. "I don't."

"You don't?"

Clearly, he'd surprised her. Perhaps with good reason, but Chelsea had heart. He couldn't fault her for that.

"What happened to Caden is a sad case. I ran into Wayne—Dr Westland—at the gym where we both work out. There's little hope of Caden recovering consciousness." He hated to tell her, but she should know the full extent of what Lacey was dealing with. Lacey. From the moment he'd met the young woman she'd reminded him of Laura. Perhaps it was her eyes, or perhaps it had been the circumstances that had brought Lacey in for that first visit. He swallowed, refocused on what he was saying. "If Caden does regain consciousness, Wayne doesn't give him good odds of ever functioning anywhere near normal. It's possible, but unlikely."

Chelsea winced. "His poor mother."

Jared nodded, still fighting his guilty memories. "Lacey's lucky she has Georgia. I'm not sure she'd make it through this if she didn't."

"She's angry at her mother," Chelsea said quietly. "Angry at the world, really."

"Georgia has stood by her through everything. She'll be there for her through this, too."

Just as he'd tried to stand by Laura, but she'd been angry as well. Angry and had known him well enough to sense something had changed during that spring break they'd been apart. Nothing had been the same between them after that.

"Lacey got pregnant during high school?" Chelsea interrupted, not knowing his thoughts were lost in the past, stuck on another young girl who'd dealt with an unplanned pregnancy, during medical school rather than high school, though.

He sighed. "I diagnosed Lacey's pregnancy the first day I worked here. She was seven months and hiding her condition from her mother," Jared said, not sure why he was admitting so much to a woman he kept insisting he wanted nothing to do with. Probably just because of the anxiety he'd felt from the moment Betty had mentioned Lacey's visit. He should have seen her, should have been there to help her, to offer his support in any way he could. "I have a personal stake in Caden's recovery. He was my first delivery in Madison when he came into the world a month early."

"Delivery?"

He raked his fingers through his hair, and distractedly answered. "We offered OB services until three years ago when we opted to stop due to liability insurance expenses skyrocketing. It just wasn't worth the cost and long hours as we're basically a family practice." He gave her an odd look. "But I guess Will would have told you that."

"Will's never enjoyed obstetrics. Delivering babies wasn't something we talked a lot about when he visited me at school."

No, none of them enjoyed delivering babies. Because of what had happened to Laura?

Quit dwelling on Laura. You can't change the past.

"You've always been close to your brother?"

"Always." She smiled. "Will has been the bright spot in my life."

"You say that as if the rest of your life hasn't been charmed."

She'd grown up in the lap of luxury with two of the most renowned doctors in the country as her parents. Although he hadn't grown up dirt poor, Jared couldn't imagine the opportunities Chelsea had had at her fingertips. Certainly Will talked of mission trips and health summits he'd attended from the time he'd been a young boy. He'd half expected his friend to follow in his parents' footsteps and go into the politics of medicine.

"You think my life has been charmed?" Chelsea scoffed, drawing his attention to her pinched expression.

"Hasn't it?"

"Charmed?" Sarcasm dripped from her embittered tongue. "Oh, yeah. A fairy tale come to life."

"What?" Her sarcasm surprised him, gave him opportunity to drive another wedge between them, something he desperately needed at the moment. The feel of her body still lingered and he wanted nothing more than to refresh that memory. "Mommy and Daddy didn't shower you with enough of their money and attention?"

Her jaw dropped. She narrowed her eyes and lifted her chin. "Something like that."

For the second time since her arrival in Madison, she stormed away from him, leaving him wondering if he'd pushed her too far in the wake of Lacey's visit and his thoughts about Laura.

Left him wondering why he wanted to go after her and make her explain the hurt in her eyes.

Somewhere in Chelsea's childhood something had gone terribly wrong and Jared was pretty sure her parents had a lot to answer for.

For that matter, so did he.

CHAPTER SEVEN

LATER that evening Chelsea sat at her desk, skimming over her lab call-back list to make sure she hadn't overlooked anyone. She hadn't. Which meant she was free to leave. Only she didn't want to go home to an empty house, and with Will in the emergency room that's exactly what she'd be doing.

An empty house reminded her of the empty mansion where she'd spent her lonely childhood. After her conversation with Jared she needed childhood reminders like she needed a hole in her throbbing head.

She usually kept her cool, kept her practiced smile on her face when someone mentioned her parents. Why Jared's remark had got to her she wasn't sure. Then again, everything about the man got to her so she shouldn't be surprised.

A knock sounded on her door, and she glanced up. Her breath caught. Minus his lab coat, Jared stood in his dark slacks and pullover that emphasized his broad shoulders and narrow hips.

She reminded herself she was irritated at him for his careless comment.

Then again, she couldn't blame him for the problems of her youth when really there wasn't anyone to blame. Her parents were wonderful doctors, but just hadn't been able to love a defective child when they'd been the ones used to charmed lives. They'd wanted her to be perfect, had been willing to pay any price to achieve that perfection, even when it meant putting her through painful procedures and therapy, even if it had meant robbing her completely of any semblance of a normal childhood. At times she'd felt they'd worried they'd be contaminated if they spent much time with her and that's why they'd traveled more often than not, doing research, mission work, striving for medical care for all. She'd been left behind with her nanny and various doctors and therapists.

But her parents did the medical community a lot of good, and she could never begrudge the world their contributions. Too bad they'd had such little compassion for their daughter, insisting on brace after awkward brace, operation after painful operation, therapy after long-enduring therapy. When they'd wanted to send her back for more cosmetic surgery at seventeen to decrease her scarring, she'd refused, not able to bear the thought of going under the blade again, not for vanity reasons, not when the surgery had really been more to do with her parents trying to turn her into the perfect person than for her.

They'd forced her to see a psychiatrist, accused her of deviant, unappreciative behavior, threatened to have her committed for therapy. Thank goodness Will had stepped in, offering to take her with him on his spring break and "make her see reason". But he'd never pushed her to have her scars removed, and had calmly informed their parents Chelsea wouldn't be undergoing any more surgeries.

Those scars were reminders of who she was, how much she'd overcome, but she'd be lying if she didn't admit they were also a source of contention. She protected those scars, only having shown willingly one person the slashes along her spine and shoulder blades. Kevin's reaction had forever ended her relationship with him.

How would Jared have reacted to the horrific vertical cuts if she had bared her soul and body to him? Would he have turned away in disgust as well?

"You're not speaking to me?" he asked when she remained lost in her own world. "Not that I blame you."

Knowing she'd never know the answer to her question, she pushed the paper she'd been holding away and met his blue gaze.

"Sorry. What can I do for you?" She kept her voice coolly professional. She didn't need or want a repeat of earlier, and she felt too tired to attempt to change his mind about her.

"Actually, I came to tell you that."

She blinked, thinking she'd missed part of their conversation. "Pardon?"

"The sorry part," he clarified, walking into her office. "I had no right to say what I did." He looked like a contrite little boy, a mischievous one who'd gotten caught with his hand in the cookie jar. "I know nothing about your childhood and shouldn't have said anything. I'm sorry, Chelsea."

What did one say to something like that? He hadn't had a right to judge her, but she hadn't expected the apology, or the look of sincerity and concern on his face.

"Perhaps I was overly sensitive." She'd dealt with similar comments in the past and had maintained a smile, not gotten upset. Jared was the difference.

"Or perhaps I judged your life based on nothing more than knowing Will and who your parents are. Not necessarily enough to make an accurate call."

"You know how I feel about my brother, and my parents are good people."

"That doesn't necessarily make them good parents, though, does it?" His gaze bored into her, refusing to let her look away.

Chelsea had quit fidgeting years ago. Actually, the bulky back braces she'd worn for months on end hadn't allowed her to fidget. But had she not had years of practice of sitting still she'd no doubt be squirming all over her seat because Jared saw too much.

She wasn't sure she wanted to answer as doing so might make him ask questions she didn't want to answer. Because no way did she want to point out her flaws. He already seemed to continuously focus on her most obvious one. Her too-wide mouth.

Self-consciousness swamped her, bringing memories of being the kid who had to watch everyone else play, the kid who sat on the outskirts, the kid who hadn't had friends until college, because who wanted to play with a freak wearing a brace that looked like something out of a horror movie?

Her parents had had her best interests at heart. She had to believe they had. That's why they'd put her through one experimental medical procedure after another and so often hidden her away from the world with private tutors.

She glanced at the papers on her desk, the words blurring.

"Look." Jared ran his fingers through his hair. "I didn't come in here to put my foot in my mouth again."

"No problem. Apology accepted," she said, without glancing at him. Mostly because she didn't think she could hide the pain in her eyes. Pain that ran deep and flowed freely at the moment, making her question why she'd ever thought she had a chance with a man like Jared. Why she'd ever thought he could look past her scars and see the person inside, the person who deserved love.

These days she rarely let her inner doubts show. At the moment she felt vulnerable, like every scar she had throbbed and was on public display beneath glaring spotlights.

"Why do I feel like I should say something more?" His soft question reached inside and touched the part of her already longing for him.

No matter how hard he tried, Jared couldn't be completely cold. Did that mean he cared? Perhaps just a little?

She pasted on a smile that quickly turned real when she realized Jared was looking at her without the usual scowl on his face. Not that he returned her smile. He didn't. But he didn't glare at her with antipathy either.

Perhaps it was better that he pushed her away because she could never show Jared her back, never risk that pain. So why the goofy smile on her face that something in his gaze was different? Not so cold?

"Go to dinner with me."

She blinked, not believing he'd asked. Not after how their last meal together had ended. However, she readily believed how quickly his scowl returned.

"I'm sorry," he backtracked, clearly regretting his spur-of-the-moment invitation almost instantaneously. "I shouldn't have said that."

Frustration at his immediate withdrawal filled her.

"Have I done something to make you not like me, Jared?"

He didn't answer, seemed to be trying to figure out how to answer.

"Because if the way you treat me has to do with what happened ten years ago, because I kissed you, don't you think it's time to forgive me? I was only seventeen and didn't have a clue on how to tell a man I wanted him. So I went with what felt right, and I kissed you. I didn't have all the facts and what I did was wrong. I admit that." Knowing she was going for broke and likely only going to embarrass herself, Chelsea met his wary gaze. "I'm not an inexperienced teenager any more. I'm a grown woman who knows what she wants. What I want is for this hot-cold treatment to end because your attitude confuses me and seems childish, considering how much time has passed."

The panicked look he sometimes got came into his eyes. "I didn't come in here to get into this."

"Why did you come, Jared? Was it really to say you were sorry?"

"Yes."

"Or did you want to see me? For some other reason perhaps?"

She expected him to get mad, to angrily leave her office much as she'd done earlier. Instead, he stood in front of her desk, looking confused, torn, thoughtful, like he really wasn't sure.

"What other reason?" he asked.

Eventually, she sighed, gave him a soft smile. "That you're as curious about me as I am about you. That you never forgot our kiss, and that's why you act the way you do around me."

"You're wrong."

"Am I?"

"All I did was ask you to dinner, Chelsea, then realized we shouldn't do that."

"Why not?"

"We work together. Our going to dinner is a bad idea."

She didn't believe him. At least, she didn't believe that was the only reason he behaved the way he did.

"OK," she acknowledged. "Romance between coworkers can be complicated, so let's forget the past, forget the attraction or whatever it is between us, and let's just be friends. Can't we be two people who work together and find a way to coexist without all this tension? It's time for you to forgive me for my youthful mistakes. I've said I'm sorry for what I did."

She wasn't. Not really. Sure, she wouldn't have kissed him had she'd known he had a girl-friend, but she hadn't known. The way Jared had looked at her that week, well, his eyes hadn't mentioned a girlfriend either.

But he had had a girlfriend. One he'd asked to marry him not long thereafter. Only Laura had been killed. Was that why Jared protected his heart so thoroughly? Because he'd lost the only woman he'd ever loved and couldn't bear to give his heart to another?

"Friends?" He looked duly suspicious. "You want to go to dinner with me as my friend?"

Did she? Yes. It's all they could ever have anyway.

"Friends have dinner. I have to eat. You have to eat. We need the air cleared between us because I'm tired of walking on eggshells around you." She shrugged. "Why not?"

"I'm not particularly hungry." Before he got the words completely out his stomach growled. Loudly. The noise had the impact of a pin popping a balloon, releasing the strain between them. Chelsea bit back a laugh, Jared's shoulders relaxed.

"So…" A smirk twisted his lips. "I worked through lunch and maybe a drop-in at my favorite sushi bar wouldn't be so bad."

Jared scrunched wet sand between his toes, wondering if he was a fool to be walking on the beach with Chelsea as the sun set.

Although he'd refused to completely let his guard down, he'd had a great time at dinner.

There had been a couple of occasions when she'd had him laughing so hard his eyes had watered. He hadn't expected her to be so funny, for him to enjoy her company so much when he knew he could never have her as more than a friend.

The desire for more hadn't gone away. Unfortunately. But after seeing how nice things could be as friends, he realized she was right.

His avoidance routine wasn't working anyway and the tension between them was problematic. Besides, avoidance was only feasible up to a certain point when they worked together and would be for the next twenty-plus years.

Twenty years. He glanced over at where she walked next to him. She held her shoes and the Gulf waters lapped at her toes with each wave that crashed on the shore.

He'd followed her back to her place and somehow they'd ended up going for a walk on the beach. He wasn't sure how exactly it had come about, but he supposed it didn't matter.

Friends shared walks on the beach so no harm done. He'd just make sure they returned to the house prior to the sun sinking below the horizon to avoid any pretense of anything romantic.

One could easily think the view along the coast near Will's was romantic, though. Jared had always admired Will's beach house on a semi-private part of the coast. Prior to Chelsea's arrival, he'd spent quite a few hours there during various cookouts and beach parties. But that had been last year. This summer Will hadn't done much entertaining. Hadn't done any now that Jared thought about it.

Chelsea's question about her brother hit him.

"Not that I'm agreeing with your assumptions about his reasons, but Will didn't entertain this summer, like he has in previous years."

Glancing at him, Chelsea asked, "How so?"

"He usually has several weekend cookouts and a party or two. He didn't this year."

Chelsea nodded, turning back toward the sea. "He's made a few comments that make me think he was seeing someone this summer. I think it was Leslie, and they were keeping it quiet."

"Will knows better than to become involved with someone from the office. Leslie, too, for that matter."

"Which might explain why they'd keep it quiet."

She had a point.

"Regardless, I don't think they're an item now. I just hope I'm not the cause of why they're not." He could hear the real concern in her voice, that she truly thought her arrival might have driven a wedge between Will and Leslie.

"If your theory is right, and I'm not saying it is, Will probably just ended the relationship before things became sticky."

"Perhaps," she admitted. The sigh in her voice caused him to glance at her again. She'd paused and was staring at the multicolor-streaked sky. Jared winced. How had the sun dipped so low without him noticing?

He glanced behind them. They'd walked farther than he'd thought. Will's house was too far down the beach to be reached before daylight failed them.

Which meant he and Chelsea would be sharing the sunset.

Friends could share a sunset, and it not be considered romantic.

Even if they'd shared one in the past that had ended in a kiss that had forever changed his life.

He swallowed the lump clogging his throat.

He glanced at Chelsea. Her face held a dreamy expression that made him want to take her hand in his, made him want to lean over and kiss her lips now, tonight, to see if she tasted as sweet as he remembered.

He shook his head, clearing his unwanted thoughts. "Let's go back to the house. We've both got to be in the office early tomorrow morning."

She looked at him in confusion, then with resignation. "OK."

Without another word to him or another glance toward the sinking sun, she turned and headed for the house at a brisk pace.

Jared watched her. He hadn't meant they had to run to the house, but perhaps she'd realized the danger of them being on the beach alone with the sun going down and that's why she walked like the devil nipped at her toes.

Actually, the surf did. Right up to her ankles and kept coming, darkening the edges of her rolled-up pants. In her haste she didn't notice an unexpectedly powerful surge. He saw what was going to happen as it unfolded before him. He jogged through the water to catch her, and caught her arm just as the water careened around them, drenching them both from the waist down. Unfortunately, he hadn't gotten a good footing before trying to rescue her and lost his balance. They both went down.

"Jared." Her eyes were huge when she sputtered at him from where they sat with the water pulling away from them.

At some point during the fall his hands had grasped her waist, pulled her to him to cushion her. He hadn't consciously done so, but his mind worked overtime as her wet body pressed against his. He didn't risk looking down because the sun hadn't gone low enough for him not to be able to see her wet shirt stuck to her chest. Already he was aware of the effects of the cold water on her body. Acutely aware.

Instinctively, he lowered his head, intent on kissing her, licking the salty water from her skin. He realized his error at the same moment Chelsea gave a little shake of her head.

What was he doing?

He let go of her, and jumped to his feet.

"If you wanted to go for a swim," she teased, obviously trying to lighten the moment, "I'd have let you borrow a pair of Will's trunks."

Appreciating her efforts to ease the strain of the moment, he laughed. "So much for my attempt to rescue you from getting soaked."

She glanced down at her plastered-to-her-body clothes. "That was a rescue attempt? I thought you were having American football fantasies and had mistaken me for a wide receiver."

Water dripping from his soaked clothes, Jared

held out his hand. "Actually, football fantasies sound better than admitting to my clumsy rescue."

She placed her hand in his and allowed him to pull her to her feet. "Did you play football, Jared?"

"I played every sport. I actually went to college on a baseball scholarship. Had I not torn my rotator cuff in my sophomore year, who knows where I would have ended up?"

Shock shone on her face. "Medicine isn't your first love?"

"Medicine is my life." As he said the words out loud he realized just how true they were. After Laura, he'd shed every aspect of his life with the exception of medicine and a few close friends like Will.

"Is sports how you got this?" She ran her finger over the scar above his left eyebrow. Her finger heated his skin, searing into his flesh.

"Basketball fight my freshman year of high school," he admitted.

"Fight?"

"Don't ask," he warned, grinning. "Just

suffice it to say that we won on the court, and off."

When Chelsea's hand slid back into his, he didn't pull away, although somewhere in the deep recesses of his brain a voice warned that friends did *not* hold hands on twilit beaches.

Still, being friends with Chelsea felt…nice.

CHAPTER EIGHT

CHELSEA floated through the next week. Their shared sushi and walk on the beach gave her hope that she and Jared really could put the past behind them and be friends. They'd had a nice meal and an enjoyable time. The conversation had been great. They'd laughed and joked. When on the beach he'd gone to kiss her, she'd stopped him because she didn't want to ruin their tentative friendship. Jared would have beat a hasty retreat had they kissed. Then where would their friendship be? Kaput, that's where and, despite how she longed for his kisses, she wouldn't risk him going back to avoiding her. The tension between them was her only source of contention at work, and she'd do whatever was necessary to resolve the problem.

"Why do you look so perky?" Leslie asked as she passed Chelsea in the office hallway. "A certain doctor coming around to your way of thinking?"

"We're just friends."

Leslie nodded. "If Jared had looked at me once the way he looks at you, I'd have jumped ship a long time ago."

Chelsea paused and stared at her pale friend. "You have feelings for Jared?"

Had she been wrong about Leslie and Will? Had Leslie had a thing for Jared? Was that what had been wrong with Leslie lately? Because although her friend hadn't missed any work, Leslie hadn't been herself. She'd become quiet, reserved, and had refused to go to lunch with Chelsea several days in a row.

"Not anymore and never like you obviously do," Leslie quickly assured her. "He's a gorgeous man, and I'm not blind. That's all."

"So you're not…?" Chelsea couldn't finish putting her thoughts into words. Leslie was so pretty and smart. She probably didn't have physical and emotional scars to turn off a man's interest. Actually, she'd thought Leslie pretty darn near perfect—for her brother. For Jared was another matter entirely.

"No, I'm not." Leslie shook her head. "I found him an attractive man when he first started at the clinic, but there weren't any sparks. I…" Her voice trailed off, and she nervously glanced around the hallway. Betty stood at the nurses' work station, but otherwise they were alone in the hallway between patient exam rooms.

"You what?"

Leslie shrugged. "We were destined to just be friends. Although I'm not buying friendship's what destiny has planned for the two of you."

"I wouldn't count on anything more than that," Chelsea mused, watching her coworker closely. The truth was plain on her face and Chelsea had a pretty good idea she knew exactly who had stolen Leslie's heart, and if her brother returned the nurse practitioner's sentiments, she couldn't be happier.

At least one of them could be happy in love.

* * *

Jared rapped on the exam room door then entered.

"Hello, Connie." He smiled at his favorite patient. "You look well."

Surprisingly, she really did.

"Are you flirting with me, Dr Jared?" She winked at him, giving a glimpse of her former feistiness, and his spirits lifted. Connie looked more like herself than she had at the end of their last visit.

"Always, Connie. Always."

The older woman smiled, her pale blue eyes lighting up with her inner strength.

She looked rested, calm, at peace. Not at all like a woman preparing to start chemotherapy the following Monday.

"I took a little trip out West. The travel was good for me. Cleared my head."

She'd gone on a trip? That's why she'd delayed starting her chemotherapy?

"Where out West?"

"The Grand Canyon. Rose and the boys went with me." Her face glowed with excitement. "Paul and I talked about going for years, but never did. I've always wanted to see the Grand Canyon."

The Grand Canyon? Interesting.

"I'm glad you felt able to go." Had Dr Goodall OK'd the trip or had Connie opted to go of her own accord?

"It's an amazing place," Connie continued, and although she looked at him Jared suspected she saw the multi-hued ridges of the canyon rather than the neutral beige of the exam room.

"You feel close to God when you stand there, looking over such a glorious sight. No wonder it's one of the seven natural wonders of the world." She paused. "Have you ever visited?"

"No." There hadn't been the money for trips like that when he'd been growing up. When he'd gotten old enough to do things on his own, Laura had been a part of his life and he'd fallen into her plans for the future. He'd…he'd what?

He'd betrayed someone he'd cared deeply for. Betrayed her and ultimately killed her. He'd died that night, too. He'd locked himself inside a protective shell and had quit living just as surely as Laura had. Why? Out of guilt? Out of love and respect for Laura? To keep himself from falling for anyone else? Since the evening he and Chelsea had tumbled into the sea, he'd wondered.

Found himself wondering if he wasn't betraying her yet again by wondering about what kissing grown-up Chelsea would have felt like.

"You'd like it." Connie interrupted his thoughts with words that sounded too close to the truth. He would have liked it, wherein lay the problem, the betrayal. "You should find a lady friend and go." She stared at him a moment, then mused, "You'd have made my Rose a good husband, but Marvin is a decent man and treats her well, even if he is as dull as a cardboard box."

Jared smiled at the older woman's description of her son-in-law and ignored her suggestion to find a lady friend. The word "friend" just reminded him of the truce he'd called with Chelsea. Could they really be just friends? For the past two weeks they'd managed to pull it off, chatting at work, going out to lunch as part of a group of their coworkers, sushi on a couple of occasions after hours, and they'd fallen into a shared coffee at the break table before starting their work day.

They were going for the gold medal in friendship.

"Thank goodness my grandkids take after their mother's side of the family," Connie continued. She had two grandsons. One twelve and the other fifteen. Jared had met them once, at their granddad's funeral. But he'd heard Connie mention the boys' rambunctious ways on numerous occasions and always with a twinkle in her eyes.

"Any child who inherited your strength is lucky," Jared agreed, directing his thoughts away from Chelsea and onto Connie. "Is Rose coming to stay with you while you have your chemotherapy?"

Connie's pupils contracted the tiniest fraction, giving Jared a sense of unease.

"After going on the trip out West with me, she's busy with the boys, catching up and such.

If I decide to take the treatments, I've got a friend who's going to stay."

A friend? The word was haunting him.

Or maybe it was Chelsea who haunted him.

Certainly, she appeared each time he closed his eyes at night and troubled his dreams.

"Your neighbor?" he asked, trying to get back on track with what he was supposed to be focusing on. "The one who bakes those wonderful pies?"

"Darla Kamakinski?"

"That's the one."

"Yes." Connie beamed, looking pleased he remembered the pies she'd had Darla bake for him.

Then what she'd said hit him, making him ashamed he had been so distracted with thoughts of Chelsea he'd almost overlooked what Connie had said. "What do you mean, *if* you decide to take the treatment?"

"I don't want to take another living tour through hell, Dr Jared. I've decided not to have chemotherapy again."

Bad vibes reverberated along his spine. Connie looked at peace with her plans.

"You're a fighter, Connie, and you can beat this. Why won't you at least try?"

Connie shook her head. "I've lived a good life and have no regrets. I've seen my Rose grown and happy. Without Paul, taking medicines that make me horribly sick just so I can stay alive doesn't make much sense."

He wished there was a truthful way he could guarantee a good response to her treatments, guarantee she wouldn't suffer the horrible side effects she'd had previously. He'd never knowingly lied to a patient and wouldn't start with one he cared about as much as he did the feisty older woman fiddling with her dragonhead walking stick.

"What about Rose? Your grandsons? You can't just give up without doing all you can, Connie. What kind of memory are you leaving them if you just let the cancer take you without even giving the medicines a chance?"

She regarded him a long time. "You really

believe the chemotherapy has a chance of working a second time?"

"I do," he immediately answered, hoping Connie would draw strength from his belief in her. "If you fight this, I think you have a good chance."

"You're not going to let me just give up, are you?"

"Not in a million years."

Weariness sagged her shoulders. "Then I guess I need to call Dr Goodall and reschedule the treatments."

"I'll do it now." Jared pulled out his cell phone and called Dr Goodall's office. "There," he said when he'd finished. "You're rescheduled to start treatments on Monday morning."

Connie nodded. "Thank you."

"I'm glad you've opted to take the chemotherapy, Connie."

"I know you are, Dr Jared. A lot of doctors wouldn't give a flying flip whether or not an old lady took treatment or not. I appreciate you caring. You're a good doctor." She patted his hand, compassion conveyed in her arthritic fingers and her watery eyes. "And a good man."

Her quiet praise jerked at his heart. "You're special, Connie."

They sat in silence, each quietly dealing with their emotions and Jared feeling awkward at how choked up Connie got him.

After a few moments pale eyes pinned him. "Don't you think it's time you found someone to share your life with?"

His eyes widened at her unexpected question. Unwilling to go into his personal life, even if Connie was his favorite patient and able to reduce him to feeling like an emotional school-boy, Jared shook his head, then placed his stethoscope over her heart. He finished examining her, refilled a mild anxiety medicine she'd taken occasionally since Paul had died, then helped her to her feet.

She used her cane to brace herself and, once steady, wrapped her free arm around him. "Thank you for all you've done for me."

"You're welcome, Connie." He gave her a

quick squeeze. "If you need anything, let me know."

He walked with Connie into the hallway and bumped into Chelsea. Her eyes met his, and his pulse rate picked up pace, stampeding wildly through his body. She looked fantastic with her dark hair pulled back at her nape, her eyes dancing brightly and her skin glowing with the light tan she was getting from evening and weekend hours spent walking on the beach.

"Hi, Jared." She flashed him a warm smile. A *friendly* smile.

"Chelsea." His throat went dry and her name came out sounding peculiar. Odd how being near her could make his mouth water and his tongue stick to the roof of his mouth at the same time.

Connie glanced back and forth between them, then perked up much as she'd looked when he'd first walked into her exam room. "Well, my, my, aren't you the sly one?" She gave him a pointed look. "Are you going to introduce me?"

"It's not like that," Jared began, not wanting Connie to get the wrong idea, but also not wanting to go into any explanations in front of Chelsea.

"Like what?" Connie's wrinkled face curved upward. "All I asked for was an introduction." She stuck her hand out toward a curious Chelsea. "Connie Black. Call me Connie."

"Nice to meet you, Connie." Chelsea clasped the woman's hand, appeared startled when Connie turned her palm upward and studied the lines on her hand.

"Ah, this one is a keeper." A knobby finger moved over the lines on Chelsea's palm, carefully studying the delicate paths. "She's endured great things and loves with all her heart. You should remember that on these long, lonely nights."

Jared wanted to sink through one of the cracks in the floor. He shot Chelsea an apologetic look, but found her pink-cheeked and studying Connie with interest.

"Dr Chelsea Majors," she introduced herself when he failed to for the simple reason he'd gone mute. At least, that was his diagnosis of the fact his mouth failed to cooperate.

Chelsea's smile grew wider, more engaging. "I'm Dr Will Majors's sister."

"Sister? Can't say I knew he had a sister, but I usually see Dr Jared." She gave Jared a look full of motherly affection. "He and I have been through a lot together."

"Oh?" Chelsea's brow rose.

"He diagnosed me with lung cancer several years ago."

"Which she beat," Jared quickly pointed out. "This little lady is made of tough stuff."

Could Connie tell he was reminding her she could beat this round of cancer, too?

"Not so tough these days."

"Yes, you are." He refused to let her think otherwise. "Connie is my inspiration."

"It's time for some young thing to inspire you." Connie glanced suggestively at Chelsea. "I'm old and past my prime."

"Hardly." He wanted to say more, but his words lodged in his throat yet again.

Connie continued to clasp Chelsea's hand, pulling it toward her. "Do you have a minute?"

Chelsea shot Jared a questioning look, and he shrugged, not sure what Connie wanted. Even more uncertain he wanted the older woman alone with Chelsea as there was no telling what she'd suggest.

"Sure," Chelsea agreed with an indulgent smile and a curious expression. "What can I do for you?"

Connie tucked Chelsea's arm beneath hers and gave her an appreciative pat. "Tell me what you think of my Dr Jared. He's a handsome rascal, isn't he? Smart, too."

Jared stared after them, wondering if he should run interference before Connie put ideas into Chelsea's head.

Then again, Chelsea had agreed that nothing would ever be between them except friendship, that the other had just been a silly schoolgirl crush.

Good, because he'd hate to lose the tentative friendship they'd forged, would hate to lose the brightness Chelsea added to his life because he'd come to look forward to seeing her each day, to hearing her laugh at something he'd said, to seeing her smile when their eyes met.

Sure, there was still physical attraction, but he liked having Chelsea as his friend.

And as long as friendship was all they shared, he didn't have to feel guilty about the past.

"So, what did Connie tell you?" Jared asked Chelsea when they bumped into each other at the copy machine late that evening. He'd been going to copy a form he'd filled out when he'd seen her copying papers of her own.

Chelsea turned, gave him an impish smile as she leaned against the machine. "I enjoyed meeting her. She seems like a wonderful person."

"She is. One of a kind."

"She told me about her husband dying a few months back."

"Paul died of a myocardial infarction. Very unexpected as he didn't have any known risk factors. Connie's not been the same since."

"She must have loved him very much."

"She did," Jared agreed. "Just as Paul loved her. They were a wonderful couple."

Chelsea looked undecided for a moment before meeting his eyes with a serious expression. "She said something that caught me off guard."

Besides hinting that he and Chelsea should be a couple? Because he had no illusions about Connie's reasons for wanting to talk with Chelsea. She'd taken one look at the pretty brunette and decided to play matchmaker.

"What did she say?"

"We were talking about her husband, and she made the comment that she'd see him again soon." Chelsea's eyes darkened with concern. "She had a faraway look, and I couldn't decide how to take her."

He sighed. He'd hoped Connie's spunk today meant her spirits were good, that she didn't feel defeated before even beginning her battle. Instead, he'd had to convince her yet again to agree to fight her cancer.

"Her cancer is back," he admitted. "A sarcoma

in her hip that's metastasized to several organs, including her liver and pancreas."

"Oh, Jared." Chelsea's eyes watered, and she reached out, placed her hand on his arm in a soothing gesture. "I'm so sorry."

Jared's gaze dropped to where she touched him, and he wondered how it was possible to feel comfort at such a simple thing as Chelsea's skin against him. Although perhaps comfort wasn't the right word, because the crazy things her touch did to his insides created havoc.

"She starts her chemotherapy on Monday. She'll beat her cancer again." He refused to consider otherwise. "If anyone can do it, Connie can."

A loud noise had both of their eyes widening. He'd been pretty sure they were the only two left in the building.

"What was that?" Chelsea asked, staring at Jared in surprise.

When they went to investigate, what they found had both of them jumping into professional mode.

Leslie lay on the bathroom floor in a fetal position, holding her lower abdomen. Sweat beaded her skin, curling the tendrils of red hair at her face.

"Leslie?"

Frightened brown eyes lifted. "I think I blacked out."

Chelsea dropped beside her friend and automatically began assessing her vitals, counting respirations and checking her brachioradialis pulse. Jared indicated he was going to get his stethoscope. "What's wrong?"

"I feel like someone's stabbing my insides with a knife," Leslie gasped. "I'm…" She paused when Jared returned with his stethoscope and a black doctor's bag.

"I'm going to undo your shirt and pants, Leslie, so I can check your stomach."

Wincing, she nodded.

Chelsea got a cold washcloth, folded it and placed it on Leslie's forehead while Jared gently positioned his stethoscope on each quadrant of Leslie's abdomen. When he went to lightly palpate, Leslie jerked, grabbing his hand to stay him.

"I need to check," he advised, keeping confidence in his eyes as he assured he'd take care of everything, that he'd make her pain go away. He'd do all he could to keep that promise. "I'll be as gentle as I can."

Leslie nodded. "Hurry, because something's terribly wrong."

"I'm not seeing any scars so I assume you still have your appendix, right?" Chelsea held Leslie's hand, closely watching his examination.

Jared had been thinking appendicitis, but Chelsea's question beat him to the punch. Positive guarding. Positive rebound pain.

"I've never had surgery."

"Help me get her to where the ultrasound machine is, and I'll check her appendix."

"An ultrasound?" Leslie's eyes looked panicked. "Are you sure?"

Jared didn't acknowledge Leslie's question because there was no doubt that they needed to see what was going on, stat.

"I'm going to call 911 and tell them we have an acute abdomen," Chelsea said as they assisted a doubled-over Leslie to the exam table.

He set up the machine while Chelsea made the call.

After applying the conductive gel, he placed the wand on Leslie's stomach, searching for her appendix. What he saw on the screen stilled his hands. Oh, hell.

"I know," Leslie moaned, her eyes pleading for understanding. "I know."

A thousand questions ran through his mind, but he had no right to ask anything that wasn't medically relevant to what was causing Leslie's pain, what had caused her to pass out. What he saw opened up a whole lot of new possibilities.

"The ambulance is on the way," Chelsea said, re-entering the exam room. Her eyes settled on the monitor and widened. "Is that…?" She stopped, clamping her mouth closed and staring at Leslie in wonder.

Leslie's panicked eyes met theirs. "Am I mis-carrying? I know miscarriage is common during the first trimester. Is that why I'm hurting so badly? Am I losing my baby?"

Jared didn't think so, but couldn't be sure. "Are you bleeding or leaking any fluids?"

She shook her head, straining to see the ultrasound screen, crying out in pain at her movements. "That's what I went to the bathroom to check, but then I passed out. I haven't felt anything." Leslie's eyes turned pleading. "Please, tell me I'm not losing my baby."

"The pregnancy isn't ectopic, and I don't see any obvious problems with the amniotic sac or the fetus."

He wouldn't go further than saying there wasn't anything obviously apparent. The sac appeared attached and viable. Certainly, the baby's heart beat strongly.

He shifted the wand, searching for her appendix. Then he found the enlarged, bulging area of her ascending colon.

"I don't think you're miscarrying," he told her. "But your appendix is going to have to come out straight away."

Thank God Chelsea had called for the ambulance.

Time was of the utmost essence for two lives rather than just one.

CHAPTER NINE

CHELSEA watched as Leslie was rolled into the operating room. Her appendix would be removed immediately and hopefully the trauma of the surgery wouldn't affect her pregnancy.

"Do you think she's going to be OK?" she asked Jared.

They sat in a private alcove with a sofa, two chairs, and a table with scattered magazines. Prior to the remodeling of the hospital it had been the main waiting room, but now served as an open sitting area just outside the hallway leading to the operating room.

"She should be," Jared reassured her, lacing his fingers with hers and gently squeezing. "She's in excellent hands. Dr Marks is Madison Memorial's best general surgeon."

Chelsea stared at their entwined hands, loving the warmth and comfort of Jared's touch, wondering if he realized he was holding her hand, wondering what his touch meant.

"The stress of surgery is so hard on a body, though," she said. "She could easily miscarry."

"It's possible."

"How far along do you think she is?"

"From the ultrasound I'd guess eleven or twelve weeks."

"She's not far enough along for a baby to survive if the surgery puts her into labor."

"No, but we'll think positive."

"Who do you think the father is?"

"That's none of my business."

"I think it's Will."

He gave her a pointed look. "Neither is it any of your business."

"You're right, of course, but—"

"But nothing. Leslie's business is Leslie's business. Don't harass her on who the father is."

"I wouldn't."

He sighed. "I know. Sorry. It's been a long day."

Although afraid to remind him they were holding hands, she brushed her thumb over the back of his hand. "I'm glad you were there when Leslie passed out. I'd hate to have had to deal with that alone."

"You'd have been fine."

"It's different when the person you're taking care of is someone you care about."

He nodded, glancing up when her brother stepped into the waiting area.

Their hands parted. Chelsea smoothed her slacks while Jared tucked his hand beneath his thigh. If Will noticed, he didn't comment. Actually, she doubted he had.

"She's already in surgery?" he asked, his gaze going to the closed doors. He looked tired, stressed. His dark hair was ruffled and his expression grim.

"Yes, just a few minutes ago." Although reluctant to leave her spot next to Jared on the sofa, Chelsea went to her brother and touched his shoulder. "Jared and I followed the ambulance. I called you the moment we arrived."

"I was at the nursing home, making rounds. I came as soon as I got your message."

"Jared called ahead and had the operating room ready. Dr Marks was waiting. Everything happened pretty fast."

"You're sure it's her appendix?" Will's eyes went back and forth between them.

Jared nodded.

"I heard…" Will's voice trailed off, and he met Chelsea's gaze. If there had been any doubt in her mind about Leslie and her brother's relationship, about who was Leslie's baby's father, the way her brother's face paled to a ghostly white would have convinced her. "She's really pregnant, isn't she?"

"Yes. Jared did an ultrasound in the office."

Jared cleared his throat from behind her, but Chelsea wasn't going to keep secrets from her brother. With Leslie so well loved within the medical community, word of her urgent condition, complicated by a pregnancy, would spread like wildfire. Actually, it sounded as though the rumor mill had already spread word throughout the hospital as her brother knew.

"What did you hear?" she asked.

"Just what your message said. Leslie was brought in with appendicitis and was being rushed to surgery. But I bumped into one of the paramedics on my way in and he mentioned Leslie was pregnant."

A big no-no as the man had had no right to deprive Leslie of her confidentiality, but Chelsea nodded. "She is."

"What did Dr Marks say?"

"He didn't. Unlike a paramedic who needs to be reprimanded, Dr Marks couldn't discuss Leslie's personal health with us. We're not family," Jared reminded pointedly. "We've called her sister, but she lives an hour away and hasn't arrived yet."

"Dr Marks wouldn't tell you anything? What the…?" Will pulled free of Chelsea's hand, heading toward the operating room.

"Will," she warned her brother, worried at the determined look on his face. "You can't go back there. We're only allowed to wait outside the OR as a professional courtesy."

"I'm going to find out what's going on."

"No." Having jumped up from where he'd been sitting, Jared grabbed Will's arm, stopping him just as he reached for the door. "I'm sure you're worried about Leslie, but you can't do any good by breaking Dr Marks's concentration."

Will glared at Jared, looking as if he wanted to slug him.

"Think about what you're doing, Will. She's in surgery. What's going to happen if you go barging in there?"

"Will," Chelsea said, afraid the two men she most cared about were going to come to blows.

Will visibly shook, his head slumping forward. "You're right. She probably doesn't want to see me right now anyway."

"She's under anesthesia. She won't know you're there even if you do go busting in. Let Dr Marks do his job."

Chelsea frowned at Jared's blunt tone. "I'm sure if Leslie was awake she'd want to see you."

Will didn't comment. Chelsea stayed at his side, talking with him, to pass the time while they waited. Jared had returned to the sofa and flipped through a magazine, but from the noisy, rapidly turned pages he couldn't concentrate any more than she could.

Leslie was pregnant.

By her brother.

She was going to be an aunt. Her parents were going to be grandparents. Wow.

Chelsea hesitated before getting out of Jared's car. She'd ridden to the hospital with him, and although she'd wanted to stay with Will, her brother had insisted she go home. Jared had reminded her that Will and Leslie needed time alone.

However, Chelsea didn't want to be alone right now and she lingered in the parking lot.

Too much weighed on her mind. Leslie and the baby had come through surgery OK. So far there was no evidence of hemorrhaging to hint at a pending miscarriage. But the fear was still there. Not only that but her brother and Leslie did have a lot to work through.

Thank goodness Jared had been with her this evening. She'd enjoyed the closeness they'd shared tonight and if she was honest with herself, she would admit that being near Jared was probably the real cause of her hesitation to leave.

"I'll follow you home."

Nodding, she got into her car, but her restlessness wasn't any better by the time she got to Will's beach house.

Jared got out of his car, but rather than head toward the house he leaned against the door.

"Goodnight, Chelsea. Try to get some rest."

She shot him a pleading look. "You could come in for a while, or we could go for a walk on the beach."

He ran his hand over his face. "I'm not sure that's a good idea."

"But we're friends, right?" She put him on the spot, knew she was putting him on the spot, and didn't care. She didn't want to be alone.

She wanted him.

"I'm trying, Chelsea."

"Trying to be my friend?"

He hesitated, then surprised her with his blunt honesty. "Trying to just be your friend and not want more. Lots more."

Telling him she wanted him to be more played on the tip of her tongue. The only thing staying her was the all-too-real fear of him going back to avoiding her. She couldn't bear losing his friendship if she slipped up.

"What do you want?" she asked, fighting the longing to beg him not to leave her alone, that she'd been alone too long, and tonight she just wanted someone to hold her close.

"To go home, get some sleep, and hope tomorrow is a better day."

Jared went home, but the next day wasn't a better one. Neither was the following Monday. The office staff juggled the appointment schedule to cover for Leslie's absence, and everyone's workload was heavy.

He'd worked through lunch and so far his afternoon had consisted of three depression patients, a diabetic who was recovering from a recent toe amputation due to gangrene, a hemorroidectomy, numerous upper respiratory patients, and the heart-failure patient he'd just finished examining.

"Dr Jared, there's a call for you on line four." Kayla poked her head into Jared's office. "It's Dr Goodall's nurse about Connie Black."

Jared finished entering the information on the heart-failure patient and hit the save key. "Got it. Thanks, Kayla."

He picked up the receiver. "Dr Floyd here."

"Hold while I get the doctor, please," the nurse immediately responded.

Jared pulled up Connie's file. She was due to start her chemotherapy this morning. Had something gone wrong?

"Jared?" Dr Goodall's voice came over the line. "I've got bad news."

Connie hadn't wanted to go through chemotherapy again. Had she changed her mind about proceeding with treatment? He'd call her, convince her to go, drive her to the appointment himself if that's what he had to do to get her there.

"Connie started her chemotherapy this morning and did fine."

Relief washed over him.

"But Connie's neighbor just called. Apparently after they got home Connie suffered a severe reaction to the medication. I've called for an ambulance and am heading to the hospital to meet them, but I knew you'd want to know."

Tension gripped the muscles in Jared's neck, clawing into his very being. He pulled his car out of the designated doctors' parking lot and onto the highway to head home.

What a hellish day.

Mere moments after the ambulance, he'd arrived at the house Connie had shared for forty years with her husband. They'd all been too late. The paramedics hadn't even attempted resuscitation. Not that a dozen attempts would have mattered.

Connie's face had already turned blue and with such a rapid onset of discoloration Jared suspected she'd had a clot that had gone to her brain, cutting off vital blood flow.

He rubbed his fingers over his face, trying to ease the gritty feel of his raw eyes. When he pulled back, moisture dampened his skin.

Oh, hell.

No. He wouldn't. Hadn't ever. Not even when his life had fallen apart after Laura had died.

He wouldn't start now. Not today. Sure, he had guilt, but didn't he always?

A horn honked and he realized the light had changed, but he hadn't moved. He let off the brake, hit the accelerator. Just a few more minutes and he'd be home.

Fatigue swept over him. He'd go to the house he'd bought the year after arriving in Madison to signify the permanence of his life there, take a hot shower, and go to bed. Tomorrow, when he'd rested, he'd sort through his reaction to Connie's death, sort through his guilt.

Yet another woman he'd cared about that he'd let down.

Only when he pulled into a driveway, it wasn't the long, winding one to the refurbished house where he lived.

The drive belonged to Will Majors's beach house.

Will, who planned to stay the night at Leslie's place to take care of anything she might need. Will, who'd waited for him while he'd told Rose the news about her mother. Will, who'd stood by him through all the stuff with Laura, encouraged him to come to Madison and buy into the practice. Will, who was his good friend and partner.

Will, who wasn't at home.

But his little sister was.

So what the hell was he doing here?

And why couldn't he bring himself to shift his car into reverse because all the reasons he hadn't been willing to much more than leave his car last week still applied and then some?

* * *

Chelsea cradled the cordless phone between her shoulder and right ear while she pulled a deli pizza from the oven. She inhaled deeply and sighed with pleasure. Not the healthiest choice but, as far as taste went, she considered pizza to be manna from heaven.

"Hey, Will, how's Leslie?" she asked, sliding the pan onto a heat pad.

Will called to check on her every night he worked in the emergency room and, although he wasn't working tonight and was likely at Leslie's house, he apparently still thought he should do so. Sometimes she wondered how he thought she'd managed while in college when they'd occasionally gone weeks without talking.

"She's doing great and goes for her first OB appointment in the morning."

"You're still planning to go with her?"

"Yes." She could hear the hesitation in his voice and became uneasy. Surely, he wasn't having second thoughts about his role in Leslie's and the baby's lives? Although he hadn't told her many details yet, he had admitted to having feelings for Leslie.

"Will, you're sure Leslie's OK?" Her friend had looked OK, better than OK really, when she'd visited her earlier in the day.

"Chels, Connie Black died today."

All thoughts of her brother and Leslie came to a screeching halt. Connie Black. The sweet little lady with the striking eyes she'd met at the office. The lady who'd asked her point-blank if she loved Jared. The lady who'd told her she should go after what she wanted because life was too short to sit around, waiting for love to happen.

Even now the feisty woman's words rang hauntingly in her ears.

"I'm sorry," she said. She'd wondered why Jared had hightailed it out of the office so quickly. Kayla had said he'd gotten a call just as he'd finished his last appointment, and he'd taken off. The call must have been about Connie. "She was to start her chemotherapy today."

"She had a reaction to her chemotherapy, threw a clot, and died instantly."

Chelsea cringed at the thoughts that must have been in Jared's head when he'd gotten the call, at the overwhelming frustration and loss he must feel at Connie's death.

"I met her once, in the office," she mused. "She seemed like a wonderful lady."

"She was."

Chelsea went to close the oven door.

"Look, Chels…" Stress deepened Will's voice. "Jared's taking her death pretty hard. I'm worried about him."

"Ouch." Chelsea jerked her hand away from the hot metal, dropping the phone in the process. Sucking on the burned finger, she picked up the phone before her brother had the rescue department on the way.

"Chels? What happened?"

"No biggie." She situated the phone back between her shoulder and ear. "I made pizza and burned my finger on the oven door."

Walking to the sink, she turned on the tap and

let cold water cool the skin, inspecting the pink area. She saw only a surface burn but unfortunately that didn't ease the pain.

"You OK?"

"I'm fine." The cool water helped. "Now, why did you call to tell me about one of Jared's patients?"

"Like I said, I'm worried about him." He hesitated. "I've never seen him so upset over a patient. He feels responsible for Connie's death and, just like with Laura's accident, he's blaming himself." Another hesitation. Very unlike her brother. "I thought you might go to his place and check on him."

Chelsea's heart squeezed. "You're kidding?"

"Why?"

"Because you've done everything you can to keep me away from Jared since I got here. I can't believe you'd intentionally have me go anywhere near him."

"Have I?" He considered her accusation as if the thought had never occurred to him, which she knew it had. The fink. "If I'd wanted to keep you away from him, I'd never have agreed to you coming to work at the clinic."

"Huh?"

Will gave a big sigh. "I know something happened between you two that spring break."

"I had a crush on him, that's all."

"He was so wrapped up in Laura during that time, but you got to him. Still do."

Will was asking her to go and check on Jared, telling her Jared was interested in her.

"Why are you telling me this?"

"Because I care about you both and any fool can see he still gets to you, too."

Chelsea had no more than hung up the phone when a knock sounded at her door. Not a very loud one and she could almost convince herself she'd imagined the noise.

Except she knew she hadn't.

"Who's there?" she asked, before releasing the safety chain. Although she was afraid to get her hopes up, she had a pretty good idea of who stood on the other side.

"Jared."

Her heart beat a rapid tattoo in her chest, making breathing difficult. Jared had come to her. Of his own free will. Maybe her brother was right. Maybe she did get to Jared. With shaky fingers she released the catch and opened the door.

Any joy she felt that he'd come to her faded the moment she saw him. He looked awful.

She stepped back, allowing him entrance, wanting to convey her sorrow at his loss, to let him know she understood and was there for him.

Only he stood on the stoop, staring at her with hollow eyes. "I'm not sure why I'm here."

"Jared." She sought the right words and didn't find them. "Come in."

Which couldn't have been the wrong words because with only a moment of hesitation he came inside.

"Sit down," she suggested, feeling self-conscious about the gym shorts and T-shirt she'd changed into after arriving home.

His gaze touched on the sofa but he didn't

move, just stood a few feet from her with his hands shoved in his pants' pockets. He looked like a lost little boy.

She couldn't stand the ache in his eyes, the aloneness that permeated him. Whatever his reasons, he'd come to her. She cared too much to ever turn him away, not when he needed her. Whether he acknowledged that need or not.

She reached out, touched his hand, and gave it a gentle squeeze. "Will called me."

His face tight, he nodded, surprising her by not withdrawing his hand. Still, she wouldn't get her hopes up that him coming there meant anything other than his sense of loss at Connie's death and him wanting to be with a friend. Will was at Leslie's so maybe that was the only reason he'd turned to her instead of her brother.

"I can't believe she's gone." Jared's gaze dropped to their hands, and his eyes glistened. "I shouldn't have insisted she have the chemo-therapy. She didn't want to. What right did I have to tell her she had to fight?"

His voice held anger, self-accusation, and a whole lot of raw pain.

"Her death isn't your fault." She softly rubbed her thumb across the back of his hand in a caressing motion. Helplessness washed over her. She wanted to ease his sorrow, to take away his pain, to comfort him however she could, yet she didn't know where to begin, what to say to lighten his burden.

"Connie knew the risks. She made the choice to have the treatments. What happened is horrible, but couldn't have been foreseen. It wasn't anyone's fault."

"She wouldn't be dead right now if I hadn't pushed her," he began, looking away when his voice broke. Moisture shimmered on his dark lashes, and Chelsea's heart pinched so tightly she could barely breathe.

She lifted his hand to her chest and hugged it to her. Words seemed inadequate when she wanted to give so much more.

They stood in silence, Chelsea wanting to comfort him, feeling the tremble in his hand next to her heart. His arm went around her, pulling her to him tightly, and he buried his face in her hair. "She's dead because of me."

"Oh, Jared," she breathed against his neck, wishing she could take away every ounce of his sorrow, every ounce of his guilt. "I'm so sorry she's gone, but you're wrong. Connie's death was an accident."

"I failed her." He rolled his forehead against hers, his face squished with torment. "I thought I knew best, that if she'd just take the treatments she'd overcome her cancer. I couldn't bear the thought of her not fighting. I should have listened to what she wanted. If I had, she'd still be here."

"You couldn't have stopped her from dying, Jared," Chelsea said. "Without treatment she would have died. Chemotherapy was her only hope."

"I know." But she could tell he didn't. Not in his heart.

She held him, not speaking, not acknowledging how he shook, how he leaned into her, his face buried in her hair.

His body shook next to hers, and his arms tightened their hold, molding her against him. She didn't care. She clung to him, knowing that next to Jared was where she always wanted to be, through the good times and the bad.

She wasn't sure how long they stood there, wasn't even convinced at first that she felt the light brush of Jared's lips against her hair. Not until he began trailing kisses over her face in what she knew was a desperate attempt to ease his pain.

Needing to take away his hurt more than to draw her next breath, Chelsea lifted her face and kissed the corner of his mouth.

When he didn't pull away, didn't remind how they shouldn't become involved because of being coworkers, didn't remind of how they were just friends, didn't complain or remind her she was too young and he was in love with someone else, as he'd done the last time she'd kissed him, she kissed him again. Only this time she pressed her lips fully to his and moaned when something within him snapped. Snapped and unleashed the flood of emotions dammed inside, showering her with his need. She welcomed the passionate storm.

He kissed her mouth, assaulting her lips until she opened, granting him access.

He kissed her with all the fervor she'd longed for when she'd first fallen head over heels for him and for what seemed like most every day since.

He kissed her until she clung to him, breathless and needy. Not at all like "just friends". Oh, no, his kisses were raw, edgy, full of passion, intense. Wonderfully intense.

"Your mouth drives me mad." He brushed his hands over her hair, her face, her lips. "I've wanted to kiss you, to feel your lips against mine. When you smiled at me for the first time, Chelsea, I wanted you. God, how I wanted you, but you were too young and I was involved with Laura. I had no right to want you. Not then, not now, but I do. I want you so much."

Chelsea stared at him, wide-eyed and in shock. She'd seen the way he looked at her. On some level she'd recognized the emotions as similar to what surged through her veins, but he'd pushed her away and she'd lacked the experience and confidence to do anything about his rejection. But Jared was admitting to wanting her. His hungry expression admitted to much more than his words said.

And he liked her mouth? He must, because he was kissing it again, devouring her lips with his in urgent caresses that told a story of their own. A story where Jared cherished her.

"You have the smile of an angel."

He was an angel.

Had to be because his kisses, his touch were heavenly.

Feeling emboldened by his praise, Chelsea stroked her fingers over his shoulders, his neck, curling into the midnight hair at his nape. The silky strands were just long enough to tangle her fingers in, wrap around her fingers, hold him to her, and show him everything in her heart. Everything that had been in her heart for what seemed like an eternity.

She had no concept of time, of how long they stood touching, caressing, comforting, not until Jared pulled back.

"I shouldn't have come here. Not like this." He raked his fingers through his hair. "I'm taking advantage of you. Of this moment. Laura. I can't."

Fear pulsed through Chelsea. She didn't want him to leave. But any second he'd go back to the pretense they'd maintained for weeks. She was tired of pretending he wasn't everything she'd ever wanted, because he was.

Tonight, at this moment, he needed her, wanted her, looked at her like she was everything he'd ever wanted. That thought was heady and one that sparked her into action.

She cupped his face, making him look at her. "You're not taking advantage of me."

"I'll just hurt you, Chelsea. It's what I do, even when I don't mean to." His gaze held hers and already she could see him throwing walls up.

"Please, don't," she pleaded. "Don't ruin what

just happened by telling me how wrong our kiss was or how we can never have a relationship because of all the bad things that have happened or might happen."

He opened his mouth, and she shook her head.

His eyes took on an increasingly tortured appearance, but he didn't move away, didn't launch into an argument on the detriments of office dating. Instead, he cradled her face and gently stroked his thumb over her cheek.

She didn't want to move, didn't want to risk him moving his hand away. Such tenderness was conveyed in his simple touch. Tenderness that said he cared and ached for what she could give him.

He eyed her with torn emotions, but what shone through was his need. That need undid her, made her resolve weak, her determination strong. Not sexual need, although lust was there in abundance. No, what she saw was a need to feel alive, to feel connected with another human being, to not be alone. She recognized the emotion well and hated it that the nasty feeling had a hold of Jared.

His thumb stilled against her face, and he took a deep breath. "Tell me to go, Chelsea, please, because I don't want to leave. God help me, I don't want to go."

"Then don't," she whispered, not bothering to attempt to hide what was in her heart. She couldn't have anyway. Not when she overflowed with love. "Stay with me. Let me hold you."

His jaw tightened. "I won't use you. You deserve better than that. I won't risk hurting you."

"I'll hurt if you leave."

He closed his eyes, torment on his face.

A thousand thoughts ran through her mind. If he left, where would he go? What would he do? Who would hold him while he fought his grief? His guilt? Would he end up shrouded behind even more emotional barricades? But if he stayed, how would she let him go in the morning and pretend nothing had happened if that's what he wanted? Because she'd never want to let Jared go.

When looking back on her life, she knew this moment would stand out as monumental. If she didn't seize the opportunity to love Jared, to give to him even if he could never give back to her, she'd regret her decision, just as she'd regretted letting him walk away after she'd kissed him all those years ago.

Laura or not, too young or not, she should have told him how she'd felt.

No matter if he used her to distract himself from Connie's death. No matter if he left her bed in the morning only to ignore her at the office. No matter if they never had anything else beyond tonight. Even if Jared took one look at her back and felt revulsion, she wanted him to stay.

She would take what fate gave, which was one moment to the next, and in this particular moment she was right where she wanted to be. In Jared's arms.

Connie Black's voice whispered in her ear, "Grab what you want and make it happen. If you love the boy, let him know. Show him what's in your heart."

She stood on tiptoe and moved to within millimetres of his mouth. His eyes had opened and raged with an inner battle between logic and need.

"I want to love you, Jared. Stay with me."

Despite reason warning he'd regret his actions, Jared wasn't going anywhere.

Not tonight.

He couldn't face the emptiness of his heart.

Was that why he'd held onto his anger at Laura for so long? Why he'd held on to his guilt? Because without it he had nothing left to feel? To make him feel alive?

At the moment he felt alive.

More alive than he'd ever felt.

Because of Chelsea.

She stared at him with such longing, such sweetness. He wanted to swoop her into his arms and protect her from the world forever.

In reality, he needed protection from her because he'd be the one to have to start over when the rubbish hit the fan, as it inevitably would.

But he wasn't leaving. Not when the tenderness in Chelsea's eyes promised that drowning himself in her heaven would be worth whatever hell he later faced.

Knowing she waited for his answer but unwilling to verbalize his weakness, he leaned in, took her mouth, and lost himself in the sweetness of her body.

CHAPTER TEN

ALTHOUGH he hadn't said a word since calling out her name in a passionate cry, Chelsea knew Jared was awake.

He'd rolled onto his side, pulled her to him, and held her close. She waited for him to notice the scars on her back, to jerk away in disgust or whatever it was Kevin had felt when he'd seen the evidence of her surgeries.

But if Jared noticed, he didn't comment, just breathed softly into her hair.

Tears stung her eyes although she wasn't sure if they were from happiness, sadness, or relief.

She loved Jared. He'd been tender and demanding and all-consuming. By no means was she an expert on sexual relations, but she didn't need to be. What they'd shared had been special.

"I should go."

So special he wanted to leave even before his breathing had returned to normal.

Chelsea stiffened, but she didn't beg him to stay.

If he still wanted to go after what they'd just shared, there wasn't anything she could say or do that would keep him with her.

"But I'd like to stay," he continued. "If you'll let me."

Elation filled her. He wanted to stay.

"I told you I wanted you to stay," she reminded him. "That hasn't changed."

He kissed the back of her head in a gentle peck, and Chelsea smiled. Everything would be OK.

Her stomach growled, reminding her of what she'd been doing when her brother had called, when Jared had arrived at the beach house.

"I have pizza and beer, if you're hungry."

"I'm starved," he admitted, brushing his lips against her hair as if he might be referring to her when he admitted to his hunger. "I missed lunch."

Taking care not to expose her back, she rolled,

stared into his eyes. "I'm glad you're here, Jared. That you came to me."

His eyes searched hers for the longest time before he nodded. "Me, too."

After reheating several slices of pizza in the microwave, Chelsea and Jared sat on her sofa, munching. Surprisingly, Jared talked almost non-stop. Mostly about Connie Black, her daughter and grandsons, her deceased husband, and what a wonderful life they'd had.

"I wish I'd had the opportunity to know her better," Chelsea said, before taking a sip of her beer.

"You'd have liked her." He picked at the label on his glass beer bottle. "In some ways you remind me of her."

"I do?"

"You're both spunky as hell."

"I'll take that as a compliment."

"I meant it as one. You both have a passion for life and aren't afraid to take risks." He placed the bottle against his lips and took a drink. "A part of me knew she'd agree to chemotherapy again if I pushed. Maybe that's why I pushed so hard for her to go. After Paul died, she went on, but wasn't the same."

"He must have been an amazing man for her to love him so much."

"They complemented each other well. Paul stood by her, gave her strength during her last bout of cancer."

He launched into another story of a visit with Connie and Paul. When he'd finished, he looked at his empty plate, the two empty bottles on the coffee table, and then at her. "You're easy to talk to. I find myself telling you things I never meant to say."

"It's not so difficult to be a good listener when I'm interested in the topic." She smiled. "And the person speaking."

His eyes darkened to a deep navy. "Where do we go from here, Chelsea? Tonight's complicated the hell out of things, hasn't it?"

"I don't see us as a complication, Jared. To me, what we share feels right."

Surprisingly, he nodded. He picked up an empty beer bottle and toyed with the paper label, peeling it away from the glass surface.

"I'll be here for you when you need me, Jared. Always."

Panic edged into his expression, and she wondered if she'd said too much. No. They'd just made love. If she couldn't tell him how she felt then she sure shouldn't have invited him into her bedroom.

"Let me help you clean up," he said, gathering up the bottles and heading to the kitchen.

Chelsea stared at Jared and wondered how she'd gotten herself into this predicament. One minute they were having a great conversation on her sofa over beer and pizza, then cleaning up her kitchen, the next they're walking on the beach hand in hand, and the next he was stripping off his shirt and asking her to go into the water with him.

No way did she want to go skinny-dipping with Jared.

Well, she did, but not when it meant he might see the long scars on her back.

Was there enough moonlight that he'd notice the scars? Had he already seen them and not cared? She couldn't buy that. Surely he'd have asked about them? She recalled his hands gliding across her shoulders, her waist, but not once had his fingers moved over her marred skin. She'd been on her back, on him…no, he didn't know.

"Don't try to tell me you're shy because I'm not going to buy it. Not after earlier."

Moonlight reflected off the water, glistening against his skin. She couldn't keep her eyes off his chest, his abs, how a fine line of hair disappeared into the waistband of his jeans. How she knew exactly where that arrow led and just how perfectly his body melded with hers.

She'd known he was gorgeous, that his body was solid and fit, but, oh, in the short time from when he'd made love to her, she'd forgotten. Or had not allowed her mind to believe that just seeing his finely muscled abdomen would make her mouth go dry and water all at the same time. She swallowed, but the motion felt more like trying to gulp sand.

His fingers lingered at his jeans snap, drawing her gaze back to the sexy arrow of hair, making her think that no anatomy lesson had ever prepared her for Jared's body.

"I'm not much of a swimmer," she mumbled above the sound of the waves.

"I've heard Will talk about the vacation you two went on last summer. He took you to the Caribbean."

"That doesn't mean I swim."

"You went scuba diving. Tell me, how did you do that if you don't swim?"

He had her there.

"Go in without me. I'm not feeling up to a swim tonight."

He sank down onto the sand beside her and stared at the moonlight, clearly trying to decipher her thoughts.

"Will's been a good brother, hasn't he?" she asked to change the subject before he pushed to find out what caused her aversion to taking a dip.

Jared's jaw flexed. "Will is a good man, so I imagine he's a good brother. Certainly, he's always seemed to care a great deal for you."

"He was my hero, growing up," she admitted, refusing to let the conversation lag.

"Did Will rescue you from dragons?"

"Oh, definitely."

Jared reached out, took her hand in his. "Were there lots of dragons in your childhood?"

At first she thought he was making a snide comment, but a quick glance in his direction revealed he was serious. That maybe he saw more than most.

"Enough to keep my brother busy."

"What about now?" His thumb caressed her palm. "Are there dragons you need rescuing from?"

She started to say no, but realized that would be a lie. Dragons haunted her every day. Leftover dragons from her childhood. Deeply embedded dragons that said she was scarred and unlovable. Dragons that said a man like Jared wouldn't really ever want her. Dragons that lived within herself.

How could one be rescued from one's self?

"I have dragons."

"Fire-breathing ones?"

"Total flamers."

"There's an entire gulf full of water, Chelsea. No dragon can get to you here." He lifted her hand, kissed it. "But I'll stay close, just in case."

Jared close?

She wanted him close. So why was he standing, watching her with dark eyes?

He stripped off his pants, leaving only his boxers to cover his hips. Chelsea refused to look up. To do so would put her gaze right at his most private parts and she just couldn't. Not when she so vividly recalled making love with him.

"Chelsea?" He said her name in a low voice. She barely heard it above the crashing of the waves.

But she knew what he wanted, what he was asking.

Her breath heavy in her chest, she slipped her fingers into his outstretched palm.

She'd take this chance, trust in what she felt for Jared.

Because deep inside she trusted him not to hurt her. Trusted that he really would protect her from the dragons haunting her.

With his free hand he undid the buttons on the casual sundress she'd slipped on after they'd made love. She'd felt oddly exposed in her shorts and T-shirt with him fully dressed in his work clothes.

He slid the strap from her shoulder. His fingers lingered, teasing the suddenly chilled skin. "You're an amazingly beautiful woman."

She gulped back that she wasn't, that when he saw the rest of her he might think differently. Instead, she waited for him to discover the truth on his own.

"I didn't think it was possible for me to feel good today, Chelsea. Not after everything that happened with Connie and my guilt, but I do." He bent, kissed one shoulder, then the other. "Thank you."

The fabric slid from her body and pooled at her ankles, leaving her wearing only her panties and her bra.

The moon was bright enough that she felt exposed, but she didn't turn away from his exploring eyes. The way he looked at her left her feeling cherished, beautiful.

And that scared her, made her feel set up for a fall. A hard one.

She had to know. Had to know how Jared would react to her back.

"I have to show you something."

His gaze lifted to hers, and he grinned. "Is this where you show me something, and then I have to show you something?"

She shook her head, fighting the panic rising in her throat. Silly, she'd come to term with her scars, had opted not to go back for more cosmetic surgery because her scars were badges of honor at what she'd endured and overcome. Yet she kept them hidden away from the world. Even before Kevin's reaction. Because no matter how much she told herself her scars weren't anything to be ashamed of, she didn't believe it. Neither did her parents.

"I had scoliosis as a child," she blurted out, needing to spill her secret.

"Lots of children have scoliosis." Jared regarded her, clearly not understanding the gravity of her confession.

"Not like mine," she denied. "I wore a brace for most of my childhood, and I'm not talking a Velcro number worn under my clothes."

"The braces must have done the trick, Chelsea, because you have wonderful posture. I've always been impressed with the grace with which you carry yourself." He ran his hands along her spine.

"Not just braces," she pointed out when his fingers paused at the tell-tale ridge of one of her scars.

She waited for his nose to curl, his eyes to go cold, for him to push her away as if he'd touched something vile, all things Kevin had done when he'd discovered her imperfections.

Jared did none of those things. His fingers continued their path along her spine, but she didn't see revulsion reflected in his eyes. Not even when he continued to explore her back and found the scarred areas beneath her shoulder blade.

"Say something," she whispered, not sure he would even hear her above the sounds of the Gulf around them but needing him to verbalize his thoughts.

"Like I said, you're an amazingly beautiful woman." The way he said the words, the way he looked at her, made her almost believe him.

"You don't care?"

"I care, Chelsea."

She lowered her eyes. There for a second she'd believed… No matter, she'd known. Deep in her heart she'd known no one would ever truly love her. Her own parents couldn't get past her flaws. How could she expect someone else to? Particularly someone as gorgeous as Jared?

"I care that you went through so much all alone."

"I had Will," she quickly corrected him, swallowing the lump of emotion in her throat. Her brother had always tried to lighten her load.

"He's all you had, though, wasn't he?" His arms tightened around her and she'd have sworn anger coursed through him.

She didn't know how to answer, wasn't even sure Jared expected an answer. He just held her to him, stroking his fingers along her spine with tenderness and comfort.

"So much makes sense now," he murmured into her hair.

Still not knowing what to say, Chelsea remained quiet, her cheek pressed against his chest, her ear to his heart, listening to the steady beat mingle with the sea sounds around them.

"Never doubt your beauty, because looking at you takes my breath away. Always has."

Dear Lord, he meant it. He'd felt her scars, seen them, and he still found her attractive. Emotion swelled inside her, threatening to burst free of her chest.

And then the perfect words came into her heart.

"I love you, Jared."

"Don't say that." The warm fuzzy protective feeling Jared had been experiencing crashed and was replaced with good old-fashioned fear. Fear the likes of which he'd never known.

Chelsea thought she loved him.

She couldn't. Not really. The only woman who'd ever loved him had been Laura, and look where that had gotten her.

"But it's true," she said, lifting her head from his chest to stare up at him. "I fell in love with you when I was seventeen."

"That was a teenage crush. You said so yourself."

"Then I never got over that crush. Because despite the fact I've tried to care for other men, even let myself get close to one, they never measured up to my memory of you." Her gaze sliced into him. "After tonight, no man ever can."

Sure, what they'd shared tonight had been

amazing, but what they shared was chemistry. A strong attraction, he wouldn't deny that, but sexual magnetism wasn't love.

When that magnetism fizzled out, they'd be left with a mess. A bigger mess than they already had. If he hurt Chelsea, he'd have nothing but a bigger hole in his chest than the one already where his heart was supposed to be. The hole that Laura's death left him with.

Because a part of him had died in that car crash with her and their unborn baby.

"I don't love you, Chelsea." Honestly, he didn't think he *could* love. If he could, surely he would have been able to give Laura what she'd needed from him. And he hadn't.

Tonight, while making love, holding Chelsea close, feeling her heart beat next to him, he could almost have believed.

In reality, guilt and grief over Connie's death had left him vulnerable, left him wanting Chelsea to love him, left him wanting to believe he could love her like she deserved to be loved.

But he couldn't and wouldn't lead her on. Not any more than tonight already had.

If he and Chelsea were lucky, they'd be able to go back to their friendship. If they weren't, he'd be looking to relocate somewhere far away from Madison, Alabama.

"Is it because of my back?"

"Your back?" he asked, momentarily confused by her question.

"My scars," she said, not quite meeting his gaze. "You made me think you didn't care, but truth is you wouldn't be the first person to not be able to love me because of my flaws."

Lord help him, he might wrap his hands around her parents' necks if he ever got the opportunity.

"You're not flawed, Chelsea. I am."

She made a scoffing noise and pulled away from him, turning so that the moonlight hit her back, illuminating the lines down her spine. Although they weren't the neatest scars he'd seen, they weren't nearly as bad as Chelsea thought. Still, to a young woman the foot-long scar and its two mates must seem horrendous.

"Perhaps you didn't get a good enough look."

"Chelsea, turn around."

With her arms crossed over her chest, she did so. Moisture glistened on her cheeks.

Damn it. He didn't want to hurt her.

"I'm sorry, Chelsea. I never should have come here tonight, because from the beginning I've known we could never be. I take full blame for what happened, for putting you in this position."

"What position would that be?" she interrupted him.

"The position of thinking you're in love with me."

"How can you be so blind?" Adjusting her dress, she shook her head. "But you're right about one thing, Jared."

"What's that?" he asked with dread, knowing he wasn't going to like her answer.

"I do deserve better." With that she spun and headed back to the beach house.

Chelsea hadn't seen more than a glimpse of Jared all week. He hadn't shown up for their morning coffee and stuck to his office when not with a patient.

But, then, so did she.

After their walk on the beach, he'd gone home. She'd hoped he'd bang on the door, demanding she let him in, demanding that she give him a chance to explain why his eyes had said one thing and his mouth something else entirely.

She'd gone to bed that night full of mixed emotions. Joy that she'd made love with Jared, that he'd looked at her with love, kissed her with love, that her scars hadn't mattered to him. He cared for her just the way she was. Wherein came the problem. Jared cared, but not enough to take a risk on loving her.

Was he afraid of being hurt again? That if he loved, something might happen to her the way he'd lost Laura? Surely he had to see the folly of that thought process.

She'd hoped the morning would bring him to his senses, but he had gone back to avoiding her, and after a few abrupt attempts to talk with him that first morning, she'd opted to give him time, to let him digest what had happened between them. Maybe if she was patient just a little while longer he'd realize how special what they shared was.

What choice did she have?

Fortunately, she'd been busy planning Will's birthday party for the following Friday night. But would it have hurt Jared to at least say hi and that he was considering what had happened between them?

He'd done nothing. Done nothing but avoid her.

She'd given him her heart, told him how she felt, and he'd run. Run from her arms, her home, her life. She suspected that if he could run from the clinic, he would.

Her eyes closed and images entered her mind of him kissing her, holding her, connecting deeply on a level that went far beyond physical, and she couldn't buy it. Couldn't believe he didn't care.

"Chelsea?"

Think of the devil…

Finally, he'd come to her. She turned, smiled at Jared, her heart soaring. Only he didn't meet her gaze, and she cursed her stupidity for getting her hopes up at his slightest attention.

"Georgia Donaldson is here and has asked to speak with you after I finish seeing her." He said the words so matter-of-factly that his tone left no room for soaring hearts or hope of any kind.

She gave a tight smile. "Did she say why she'd like to speak with me?"

"I assume it has to do with Lacey and Caden, but I didn't ask."

"Because you don't want anything to do with me?" She hadn't meant to say anything. Hadn't meant to confront him. Now that she had, she realized just how hurt she was that he was ignoring what had happened. She wanted a reaction. Even if his reaction wasn't the one she longed for. Anything was an improvement over his avoidance.

Although it hadn't been easy, she'd faced her

demons, willingly shared her secret affliction, her heart. And despite the fact he cared for her, he didn't care enough to fight for her.

Which put her right back to where she'd been her whole life. Craving the love of someone who wasn't willing to give it.

"Chelsea," he began, still not meeting her eyes.

The coward.

"Don't bother." She held up her hand to stop his excuses. "Just don't bother because I'm not in the mood for more excuses on why you can't care for me. Not right now."

"Hello, Mrs Donaldson." Checking her frustration at the doorway, Chelsea greeted the tired woman waiting in Jared's exam room. "Dr Jared mentioned that you'd like to speak with me."

Dr Jared who'd looked guilty in those seconds before she'd spun and walked away.

"Yes." The woman nodded. "And do call me Georgia, please. You were so kind to Lacey when she came in a while back, I wanted to thank you."

"You're welcome, Georgia. How is Lacey?"

"Much better than when she was here." A huge smile split the woman's face. "Caden recovered consciousness last week."

Although she'd have thought it impossible moments before, joy filled Chelsea's heart. "Oh, Georgia, that's wonderful news."

"Yes, Dr Westland advised us not to get our hopes up, but he's changed his tune in the last couple of days. Caden's responding to questions by blinking his eyes. They're weaning him off the ventilator and his oxygen saturations are holding."

Chelsea's eyes watered. "A miracle."

"Yes, we think so." Georgia glanced around the exam room. "I think you made a real difference for my daughter."

"Thank you, but I was just doing my job."

"Lacey knows you were the one to arrange for the social worker to come and see her."

"I hope she was helpful."

"Extremely. She helped sort through a lot of

paperwork we didn't understand and to fill out forms so Lacey wouldn't lose her jobs. We'll forever be grateful for all you've done."

They spoke for a few more minutes.

"Well," Georgia said, "I don't mean to keep you from your patients, but I wanted to thank you for what you did for my daughter. Dr Jared, too. His visits to Caden at the hospital really meant a lot to Lacey and I."

"Jared came to the hospital?"

Georgia nodded. "He's come by every day to check on Caden. Such a good man."

Chelsea bit back a sigh. "Yes, he is." She hugged the woman and asked her to pass along her good wishes to Lacey. "I'm so happy for your family."

Smiling, she walked out of the exam room with Georgia, watching her head toward the checkout desk. She turned, and her gaze collided with Jared's.

"You knew," she accused, realizing there was no way Georgia hadn't told Jared about Caden's progress. But, then, he'd have known from his daily visits even before Georgia had come into the office today.

Jared shrugged as if not telling her was no big deal. "Georgia wanted to be the one to tell you."

"I'm very happy for Georgia and Lacey. Caden, too."

His eyes searched hers. "We all are."

Why did he just keep staring at her and making small talk? Why didn't he admit he cared? She could see it in his eyes. That he hated the awkwardness between them as much as she did.

"How about you?" she asked. "Are you doing OK, Jared?"

"Fine. If you'll excuse me, I've got a patient waiting."

But he didn't walk away, just stared at her with longing.

Longing like he'd missed her this week and didn't want to let her out of his sight.

How could he just stand there when her heart practically was bursting with emotion?

She stepped forward, planning to push him into his office and have it out once and for all.

That's when it hit her.

She'd told Jared how she felt and believed he felt the same, despite him not being willing to take a chance on them.

Knowing wasn't enough.

She needed Jared to be willing to take those risks.

To love her and be willing to fight for her, to put her above all else.

She'd spent her whole life craving her parents' love, doing all she could to try to earn their love, and the reality was that nothing she'd ever done had been good enough because they weren't willing to let themselves love her.

Did she really want to spend her life with a man who did the same?

She spun on her heel and walked away, taking a trip to the bathroom to collect herself before going into the next exam room.

For the first time in her life she looked in the mirror and saw someone lovable staring back.

Someone who deserved more than a man who wasn't willing to give her his heart.

CHAPTER ELEVEN

CHELSEA glanced around the hotel ballroom she and Leslie had transformed with streamers and balloons. Will might know about his party, but he didn't know all she'd planned. For instance, he had no clue she'd invited several of his med school buddies and quite a few were flying in for the event.

Planning her brother's party had provided the perfect distraction from Jared's continued avoidance. Not that she attempted to see him or spend time with him. She avoided him just as determinedly and threw herself into the party preparations.

Not so surprisingly Leslie joined in the arrangements with just as much gusto. Leslie would return to work the following Monday and swore that planning Will's party was the only thing keeping her sane.

Although Will and Leslie were still working out the details of their relationship, Will had practically moved into Leslie's apartment.

For the first time in her life Chelsea welcomed being alone and had decided to forge a personal life for herself in Madison with or without Jared.

She deserved a man who wasn't afraid to love her with all his heart, and the only way she'd ever meet one was to look. She planned to start…she just couldn't bring herself to start yet, but it would be soon.

What if she never met someone else she could love with all her heart, the way she loved Jared?

No, she wouldn't consider that because the thought was too depressing.

But after carrying Jared in her heart for ten years, she didn't have much hope of falling for someone else.

"What time are you supposed to meet your brother?" Leslie asked, tying off a black balloon. Although most of the room boasted brightly colored decorations, they'd opted to adorn a table just for Will with black crêpe paper, streamers, and balloons. As a gag, Chelsea had bought a silver crown and pasted a Birthday Boy sign across the front.

"At six." She watched Leslie tape the balloon to Will's special table. "I'll have him here by six-thirty."

"The guests are arriving at six?"

"Yes." Chelsea smiled at her friend. "I really appreciate you playing hostess until I get back with my brother."

"My pleasure." Leslie's cheeks brightened. "Will's a wonderful man, and I'm sure he'll appreciate all the hard work you've put into this for him."

"Hey, you've worked just as hard," Chelsea reminded her, giving credit where credit was due.

"It wasn't any trouble." Leslie's gaze traveled around the room with pride. "Everything looks great, doesn't it?"

"I couldn't have done this without you."

"My pleasure. I'd have gone crazy if I'd had to sit at home doing nothing a moment longer. Will won't let me lift a finger. I'm pregnant, not an invalid." She didn't meet Chelsea's eyes and her voice held an odd, dissatisfied note.

Were things not going well between her brother and Leslie? They loved each other. She knew they did. But, then, she was convinced she and Jared cared for each other, too, and just look at how far apart they were. Still, things would work out for her friend and her brother. They were expecting a baby and would find a way through whatever differences they were having.

A baby. Chelsea's hand went to her abdomen. What would it be like to have Jared's baby growing inside her? For his lovemaking to have given her a child?

It was possible. Although she wasn't certain, she didn't recall him having put on a condom. Yet surely he wouldn't have risked making her pregnant when he so obviously didn't want to have anything to do with her.

"You'd better go home and get dressed," Leslie said, not commenting on where Chelsea's palm rested or the faraway look she knew had settled into her eyes.

"All I need to do is slip on my dress. No big deal."

"Yeah right." Leslie smiled knowingly. "There's going to be a certain doctor here tonight I know you want to impress."

"There's nothing between Jared and I. We went to lunch a few times and tried being friends," Chelsea admitted, hoping her cheeks didn't reveal what else they'd done. "But he reconsidered even that, and I'm tired of waiting. I'm through with him," she murmured bravely, hoping that to verbalize the words could convince her heart.

"Oh, Chelsea, I'm sorry," Leslie sympathized. "I'd hoped things would work out with you and Jared. He's a fool if he can't see what a wonderful woman you are."

"I'm OK." And she would be. With or without Jared, she'd manage just fine. Somehow.

* * *

Jared finger-combed his still damp hair. He'd grabbed a quick shower and change of clothes after leaving the hospital.

Lacey had looked good. For the first time in weeks he'd heard her laugh. She'd had reason to. Caden had spoken his first word today. "Mommy."

The entire hospital had cheered at his major step in overcoming his injuries.

In many ways, Jared felt as if he, too, had won a victory in the boy's remarkable recovery. In his mind he'd tangled up Lacey and Caden with Laura and their baby. Silly, as Laura had only been five months pregnant at the time of the car crash. But in his mind Lacey and Caden had been his second chance. His opportunity to make right what wrongs he could.

Caden had a long way to go, and he might never run any marathons, but with each day he regained more and more use of his body. With therapy, the boy would walk again.

Lacey wouldn't have to live with the guilt that Jared did day in and day out.

He sighed, his gaze landing on Will's special place of honor. His pal would get a kick out of his sister's efforts. She'd decorated the ballroom with gusto, seeing to every last detail.

Chelsea put her whole heart into everything she did.

And she'd said she'd given her heart to him. That she loved him.

Perhaps she believed she did.

But he wasn't the right man for her. Just look at what a mess he'd made with Laura.

When he'd held Chelsea, felt her uncertainty, her doubts in herself, he'd known he had to put distance between them. He'd understood why Will protected her, wanted to spoil her, wanted him to stay far away. Chelsea deserved a wonderful life, a wonderful everything, because she *was* wonderful.

She deserved to be loved and cherished. Things he'd lost the ability to do a long time ago. How could he love and cherish another when doing so would be like slapping Laura's memory in the face?

"Jared? Good to see you." Tom Meeks, one of his and Will's colleagues from medical school, slapped him on the back, startling Jared from his thoughts.

Not once had he considered that friends from medical school would be at the party. Leave it to Chelsea to go above and beyond the call of duty for her brother's party and invite friends from her brother's university days.

"Tom."

They chatted, making small talk about their practices, the pitfalls of HMOs, and carefully avoided any mention of Laura. Jared glanced around the room, spotted several more of his and Laura's friends, and felt his muscles clamp inside.

There would be no escaping the past tonight.

"Why do we need to stop by a hotel?" Will asked, his face split in a grin because he knew exactly where she was taking him and why.

"Have you ever eaten at Dailey's?" She pulled the car up in front of the hotel so the valet could park it in the garage. There was a freebie lot to the side, but she didn't want to risk Will recognizing any of the vehicles. Or seeing the North Carolina number plates from the friends who'd driven down. "I hear the food is fabulous, and they have karaoke on Thursday nights."

"Too bad it's Friday and we missed karaoke, huh?" Dimples dug into his cheeks. Neither of them could carry a tune if their lives depended on it.

She handed the keys to the valet, walked round the car, and linked her elbow with her brother's. "I thought we'd check out the food and scope the place, see if we'd have any competition if we came back on Thursday."

Will laughed, escorting her into the lobby. "Scoping out the competition, huh?"

A pretty girl working behind the reception desk winked conspiratorially, letting Chelsea know she'd buzzed Leslie the moment they'd pulled into the hotel drive.

So far, so good.

When Will went to turn toward Dailey's,

Chelsea paused. "Let's go this way. I need to take a toilet break first."

"There's a bathroom in Dailey's."

"Yeah, but there's probably a line."

Will gave her a doubtful look.

"You have no idea how women's restrooms can be. Please." She squirmed appropriately to show her urgency.

His eyes twinkled, saying he knew what she was up to. "OK, go ahead. I'll wait here."

He really was a fink. "Go with me."

"To the ladies' room?"

Chelsea rolled her eyes. "A woman shouldn't run around alone in a hotel on a Friday night. It's just not safe."

He shook his head, fully aware of what she was doing, but he followed her obediently.

Of course, she never made it as far as where the signs indicated the restrooms. She grinned at him and pushed open the door to a large conference room.

"Surprise!" she said, just as chaos broke out in the room, with confetti, ribbons, and lots of cheers.

"You didn't have to fake the…" He paused, seeing how packed the room was with people. "Wow. What bank did you rob to get all these people here?"

"No bank. No paying off the guests. Just a few phone calls."

"Surprise!"

"Happy Birthday!"

"Woohoo, Will!"

Shouts went up all around them.

Will grinned, clearly pleased with the turnout of his friends. Just wait until he saw everyone she'd invited.

"Is that Larry Bowles?"

He'd seen. She smiled. He'd be ecstatic at seeing his old university buddies. But when his gaze met hers, he didn't look pleased.

He looked worried, perhaps a bit panicked, and Will never panicked. Never. Except during Leslie's appendectomy.

Unease fluttered in Chelsea's stomach.

"Is that a bad thing?" She'd been sure Will would be excited she'd brought the gang together. Will, Jared, Larry, and Tom. They'd been so close during their university days. The summer she'd met them she'd been envious of their friendship. At that time she'd just begun coming out of her isolation and had literally had no one other than Will.

So why did Will look upset about seeing his friend?

Well-wishers surrounded her brother, and he didn't get the opportunity to answer.

Chelsea stepped back, wondering why he'd looked concerned. Surely she'd been mistaken at his odd reaction.

Chelsea's laughter haunted Jared no matter where he stood, no matter how many people stood between them.

In a room full of guests that included several he should be quite aware of, how could he be so in tune with Chelsea's exact location, with everything about her? He'd swear he could even smell her perfume from time to time. That fresh-baked cookie scent that troubled him day and night, just as memories of making love to her haunted him.

He sniffed the air, then shook his head in self-disgust.

Insane.

He'd had enough and just wanted to get out of this room full of raw nerves.

The room was like a pit of vipers in his emotional state.

Jared headed toward the door. So what if it was barely after eight? This was one party he wasn't staying for. He'd wish Will a happy birthday, then he'd go home.

He hadn't been in the mood to party for weeks. Months.

From the moment he'd discovered Chelsea was joining Madison Medical Center.

He wanted her.

Deep down he admitted he'd only wanted her from the moment she'd stepped back into his life. Maybe he'd fallen for her long before that, while listening to Will.

The reality was, Chelsea deserved better. She

deserved a man who could give her his whole heart and cherish her every day for the rest of their lives. He wasn't that man. His heart had been defective since Laura and it wasn't fit to give to any woman.

His gaze shifted to where Chelsea was talking with a group of nurses from the hospital.

God, he'd missed her this week. Had fought the urge to pull her into his arms a hundred times at the office, had wanted to ask her if he'd dreamed how magical their lovemaking had been. He couldn't even be around her without wanting to touch her. Which was why he'd done his best to stay away. Far away.

He couldn't touch. Couldn't want. Couldn't lead Chelsea on when he wasn't willing to give her what she wanted.

She tossed her head back and laughed at something said to her.

Jealousy shot through him with lightning force.

Despite her words of love, she wasn't his and never would be.

Her eyes lifted, met Jared's.

She held his gaze for seconds that beat between them like a living pulse.

Was she purposely goading him?

No, Chelsea didn't play games. Her look said that if he wanted her, he must come and get her and not care that all their friends and colleagues were present. She wanted him to acknowledge her. To acknowledge that he wanted her.

He wanted.

Desperately.

Knowing he needed to retreat, Jared headed toward the exit.

"You're not leaving so soon, are you?" Leslie came up, halted his escape, and gave him a quick hug.

He just wanted to wish Will well and leave.

He wasn't enjoying this party and felt more like he was the *piñata* everyone poked at than a guest.

"It's been a long day." He paused, thinking Leslie looked tired herself. "How are you doing? Everything OK with the baby?"

"My obstetrician says everything is perfect." Leslie placed her hand over her flat lower abdomen. "My surgery didn't affect this little guy at all."

Leslie chatted on about what the obstetrician had told her and about her first ultrasound other than the one Jared had done. He tried to pay attention to their conversation, but his gaze wandered back to where Chelsea's arm was linked with that of a respiratory therapist known for being a player.

The local band Chelsea had hired played a slow number and they headed to the dance floor.

"Excuse me." Without waiting for Leslie to respond, Jared cut in on the couple's dance. Chelsea's eyes widened. The therapist looked ready to say something, met Jared's glare, then bowed out without a word.

"We need to talk."

Chelsea sent the man an apologetic glance. "You'll understand that whatever you want will have to wait as I was dancing with someone."

"Chelsea," he ground out, wondering what the hell he was doing, wondering why he couldn't stand the sight of her in another man's arms.

"Unless it's an emergency, that is," she added, her eyes daring him to take up her challenge.

"It's an emergency." Without consciously considering what he was doing, he placed his hand on her lower back and pulled her to him. "Why are you dancing with him?" he growled near her ear.

Chelsea's arms slid around his neck and she leaned close. "Give me a reason why I shouldn't."

He groaned, breathing in her fragrance, feeling the heady impact of holding her all the way down to his toes.

"I can't," he ground out, determined to keep his head.

Her cheek brushed lightly against his jaw.

What could he say? And, Lord have mercy, the light feel of her cheek brushing against him was doing funny things to his insides.

He knew he needed to say something, but he couldn't think.

He blamed his inability to focus on the feel of her body. Not in his wildest dreams had he imagined he'd actually ever hold Chelsea again, breathe in her warm scent from so close, experience again how her body felt, pressed against his. No wonder he couldn't think.

They bumped into another couple and Jared started to apologize then saw who the couple was, and nodded instead.

Chelsea watched him, her honey-brown eyes thoughtful.

"Will seemed upset that Larry was here. You don't look overjoyed. You were so close that spring break." Chelsea pulled back, stared up at him. "Is there something I should've known that I didn't?"

What could he say?

"Larry was in love with the girl I was dating when you and I met. He blamed me for her death." The admission slipped from his mouth. Somehow he'd thought that saying the words out loud would sting, would bring back old memories. He felt nothing. Nothing but sadness for a life that had been lost too young, sadness that Laura had died upset, that their baby had died, because he would have been a good and faithful husband and a good father.

But caring for him had ultimately destroyed Laura.

If he really cared about Chelsea, he'd stay away from her.

Chelsea stiffened, her smile fading. "You were engaged when she died. I remember Will telling me when you got engaged. My heart nearly broke, but when she died I mourned for your loss, Jared."

"A part of me died when she did," he admitted.

Why had he said anything? He'd totally ruined the moment, and he'd probably never hold Chelsea again. Way too risky. So why had he spoiled the magic of just having her heart next to his? Was he trying to hang on to his guilt over Laura's death? Over the death of their baby?

Chelsea bit into her lower lip, regarding him. "You loved her that much?"

"I loved Laura from the day she moved into the house next door to mine. We were in the first grade." True, but that love had been more about deep friendship toward the end. Which was why he'd felt so guilty over the way he'd reacted to seventeen-year-old Chelsea. In many ways he'd betrayed Laura—unintentionally, but a betrayal all the same.

Color heightening her cheeks, Chelsea shook her head. "Why didn't you tell me? When we met, you never acted like you were taken. I was young and naïve and totally out of my league where you were concerned. But if you'd hinted that you were in love with someone else, I never would have made such a fool of myself. Why didn't you say anything?"

"I should have mentioned Laura, but the truth is I'm a guy. Right or wrong, I liked your attention."

"You let me fall in love with you, broke my

heart." Her gaze lowered and long, soot-colored lashes shielded her eyes.

"I was a jerk. Still am."

"I was a joke to you, wasn't I? My affections a way to amuse yourself?" Disenchantment and hurt shone in her eyes.

"Never," he told her, lifting her chin so she had to look at him. "You were a beautiful young woman. You still are. I was flattered by your attention."

Her eyes searched his and he could see her remorse even before she whispered, "I'm sorry, Jared. Sorry you lost Laura. Sorry I put you in an awkward position all those years ago. Sorry I've made things awkward for you now by inviting Larry."

"Don't be sorry." He stroked his thumb over her chin. "I'm the one who's sorry. I shouldn't have flirted with you."

He *had* flirted with her, but he hadn't been able to stay away. He'd sought her out, wanting to hear her laughter, see her smile, feel the way his heart raced when she was near. All things he'd had no right to feel when he had been in a relationship with Laura. Laura. His eyes closed as he recalled the lovely girl he'd first given his heart to. She'd been his friend, his lover. Until he'd met Chelsea he'd never questioned spending his whole life with Laura, had never imagined there could be more than what he and Laura had shared.

Chelsea had shattered that illusion and no matter how hard he'd tried to make things right between him and Laura, he hadn't been able to. The truth was that if Laura hadn't beaten him to the punch, told him she was pregnant, he'd have told her how he felt, that he wanted to see other people. For ten years he'd carried that burden in his heart, keeping all other emotions locked out.

He'd used his guilt, his loss, his pain to shield him from letting anyone else close. From letting thoughts of Chelsea seep in.

He needed to think of her as his enemy.

He was dancing with the enemy.

"How is it we've caused so much hurt,

Jared?" She leaned her head against his shoulder and swayed to the music. He called himself every name in the book. What had he been thinking, to take Chelsea in his arms for a dance?

But she felt so good against him. Smelled so good.

"What are you doing, Jared?"

Nuzzling her hair. "Nothing."

"I don't think this is a good idea," she whispered roughly.

"I'm sure it's not," he agreed, with another brush of her soft hair against his jaw.

A determined glint shone in her eyes. One that made him want to lower his head and kiss her. "Stop, Jared. I don't want you touching me that way. Not when you don't mean it."

He closed his eyes, willing his fingers to relax from where he tightly gripped the fabric of her dress.

"What do you mean?" he breathed close to her ear, knowing she was baiting him.

"I want someone who isn't ashamed of me."

Is that what she thought? That he was ashamed of her? Didn't she understand all the reasons he had to stay away from her? For both of their sakes?

"I'm not ashamed of you."

"Yes, you are."

"You're a beautiful woman, Chelsea. Inside and out. Your back doesn't bother me." He grazed his fingers over where her scars ran, wishing he could soothe the deeply entrenched scars in her psyche.

"After years of being ashamed myself, I find humor in the fact I believe my back really doesn't bother you." She snorted. "All this is because of her, isn't it?"

"Laura? She has nothing to do with anything."

"She has everything to do with why you won't take a chance on me," she scoffed. "You can't let go of her. Even though she's been dead for almost ten years, you refuse to move on with your life."

"Chelsea." He breathed her name against her hair. "I have moved on with my life."

He had. He'd finished medical school, had a

great career, great friends, a life he enjoyed. That was moving on, wasn't it?

"Yet my guess is that you've not been close to a woman since Laura."

"There've been women in my life."

"I'm not talking about sex, Jared. I'm talking about a real relationship. One where you let yourself actually care about another person."

"I care…" He paused, unsure what he had been going to say. That he cared about her? He did, whether he wanted to or not.

Her gaze narrowed, and she shook her head. "Why did you pull me onto the dance floor?" she asked, no longer moving to the music. She faced him with anger in her eyes. "I want more than a few stolen kisses when you're having a weak moment. I want a real relationship with someone who is willing to trust me with his heart, who is worthy of me trusting him with my heart."

"Chelsea—" he began, but she stopped him.

"Don't 'Chelsea' me. If you're not man enough to admit you care for me and to act on those feelings, do me a favor and stay away."

With that she turned and walked away, her back eloquently straight.

Frozen in place, Jared could only watch her go. He couldn't go after her, because she was right. He should stay away from her.

CHAPTER TWELVE

CHELSEA tried to keep a smile pasted on her face as she stared across the dance floor at where Jared stood with a couple of his and Will's old college buddies.

How could she fight a ghost? The reality was she couldn't. Jared had loved Laura, had been going to marry her. He'd loved her enough to want to spend the rest of his life with her, to give her his name.

Jealousy scorched Chelsea's stomach. Totally unreasonable as the woman in question had died a tragic death, apparently taking Jared's heart with her.

Did he think he'd betray his true love's memory if he opened his heart to her? That she wouldn't be able to take it if he wasn't able to love her in return? Or was he honoring Will's request to stay away from her?

No doubt Will would go after Jared if he thought he'd hurt her in any way, which was why she could never let her brother guess at what had transpired between her and Jared.

Chelsea sought out her brother, who was dancing with Leslie. Her forehead wrinkled. Leslie didn't look happy, neither did Will. Were they arguing?

She'd wanted tonight to be perfect, but since when had life gone perfectly?

Automatically she glanced at Jared. He stood talking with Larry still. Larry's gaze shifted to Chelsea. He said something to Jared, then glanced back.

They were talking about her.

Were they having a laugh at her expense? Perhaps Jared was telling him how she'd mooned over him like a lovesick puppy for months, just like she had the week they'd met.

No more. Kevin had humiliated her with his rejection of her physical appearance, and she'd allowed Jared to repeatedly do the same thing. Only worse, Jared had rejected her heart.

Never again.

She wouldn't settle for less than the best, wouldn't allow Jared to string her along when he'd never be willing to give her his heart. Although perhaps not the life she'd have chosen, she would have a good life and find a way to be happy.

Jared stole a few private moments with Will in the far corner of the ballroom. Music played, people laughed, danced, and made merry. He and his pal both wore dark scowls.

"Women!" Will said under his breath.

"I hear you," Jared agreed, taking a swallow of the beer he'd been nursing since Chelsea had walked away from him.

Will's eyebrow rose. "Oh? Something you want to talk about?"

"Probably no more than you want to talk about what's going on with you and Leslie," Jared admitted, evading Will's question.

"She refuses to marry me," Will ground out, surprising Jared by the admission. "I've asked her a dozen different ways and the stubborn woman says no each and every time."

"I thought…"

"Yeah, well, that's two of us that thought that way. I want to get married now, sell the beach house, and get some place suitable for raising a baby."

Sounded reasonable to Jared.

"But she says no. That just because she's having my baby doesn't mean she has to do things my way."

"What does she want?"

"That's the hell of it. She won't tell me. Even tonight, I asked her to tell me what it'll take to convince her to marry me. She just shook her head and walked away from me. When she came back from the bathroom I could tell she'd been crying. I just don't understand women."

"Me neither."

"My sister giving you problems?"

Jared winced. The last thing he wanted was to talk to Will about his little sister.

Will gave a snort. "Do you think I don't know what's going on between you and Chelsea? That I never knew something happened between the two of you that spring break?"

"Nothing happened," Jared quickly denied.

"Something did." Will wiped his hand down his face. "Chelsea fell for you like a ton of bricks."

"Laura…" he started, but couldn't finish.

"Laura loved you, and you loved her, but you and I both know that you hadn't been 'in love' with her for a long time."

"You're wrong."

"I was there that spring break. Even at seventeen, Chelsea hooked you. I never said anything because I wasn't worried. I knew you. You wouldn't touch Chelsea, not without breaking things off with Laura first. I figured I had some time before I had to play big brother."

Jared gripped his bottle tight, not liking it that he'd been so transparent.

"If Laura hadn't gotten pregnant, you'd have

broken things off and when Chelsea turned eighteen…" Will's voice trailed off.

"But Laura *was* pregnant, and I did love her." They'd experienced so many firsts together, had planned on spending their lives together. He'd had no right to want someone else, to want Chelsea.

But he had.

Will nodded. "I know you loved her. We all did. Laura was a great girl. Sorry I brought her up, but I just hate seeing you so miserable after all this time."

"I'm happy," he insisted.

"Then why do you keep staring at my sister like she's everything you've ever wanted?"

"You're wrong." That would be…wrong. He'd made a promise to Laura, a promise he wouldn't break.

"If you say so, pal." Will looked thoughtful. "But Laura wouldn't have wanted this, you know."

"This?"

"You beating yourself up because she's gone."

"I'm not beating myself up."

"No, you're punishing yourself for not loving her the way she loved you, punishing yourself because you're in love with my sister."

"You've drunk too much."

Will glanced down at his glass. "Unless someone's spiked the punch, I'm completely sober. And I doubt that less than half a beer has affected you, so do yourself a favor and go grovel or whatever the hell you have to do to make things right." Will's gaze shifted to Leslie. "It's what I plan to do."

"You're telling me to go after your sister?"

"What the hell do you think I brought her here for?"

"I specifically recall you warning me off her."

"You'd have been mad if I told you I was matchmaking."

"You want Chelsea and me together? Even knowing what I did to Laura?"

Will shook his head. "What you did to Laura? What *did* you do to her? You loved her enough to sacrifice your own happiness to give her what she wanted. You."

"I killed her."

"Nobody killed her. She lost control of her car and crashed. It was an accident."

"No, she…"

"She what? Crashed on purpose? You don't really believe that, do you?"

Jared didn't answer.

"Laura was a fighter, a go-getter. Even if she was mad as nails at you, she wouldn't have done that. Not to mention that she loved you, Jared. She'd never have intentionally crashed because she wouldn't have been willing to put you through the guilt you've felt over her death."

Will's words beat against his heart like raindrops on a glass pane, rising in intensity until a thunderous downpour stormed against the wall protecting him.

He glanced up, caught Chelsea's eye from across the room. The wall cracked, emotions flooding through him.

And this time when he headed for the door, he didn't let anyone stop him.

* * *

Jared sat in Chelsea's driveway, staring at the darkened windows. So many emotions poured through him, making him feel like his blood boiled, like he needed to calm down.

He hadn't wanted to go home, knowing the quiet would drive him crazy. He'd driven around for hours, battling the turmoil within him, sorting through memories he'd never willingly let into his head.

When all was said and done, he'd ended up sitting in Chelsea's driveway, staring at her house, knowing she was alone inside. He hesitated, knowing memories of Laura hadn't been the only thing that had caused him to push Chelsea away. Fear of what losing her would do to him kept him immobile.

If he kept her at arm's length, if he refused to admit how much she meant to him, then he'd foolishly believed she couldn't hurt him.

In the process he'd hurt them both.

He'd loved Laura, and had tragically lost her. He'd have given his own life if she and their baby could have survived that car crash. But he hadn't been given that choice.

Guilt had ridden him hard, shielded him from letting anyone else get close.

The pain he'd felt at losing Laura and their baby had left him a broken man. But losing Chelsea…he wasn't sure he could survive that if he ever opened his heart.

Whether he'd acknowledged her presence or not, Chelsea had been in his heart for ten years, since the moment she'd touched her innocent lips to his in the most earth-shattering kiss of his life.

And if fate hadn't intervened, he'd have been on her doorstep the day she'd turned eighteen.

So why wasn't he traipsing up those steps and knocking on her door, begging her to let him in?

Because he feared rejection. Why would Chelsea care about him? She was a beautiful, intelligent, witty woman with a bright future. Way too good for the likes of him.

He sighed, getting out of his car and closing the door. Still he hesitated, gazing up at the clear night, the sounds of the Gulf waves crashing against the shore playing a tumultuous song.

He walked round to where the steps led up to the main level of the raised beach house, stopped halfway up to stare at the sea. Here, with the closest house several hundred meters down the coast, one could imagine being the only person on earth.

At times he'd *felt* like the only person on earth.

The loneliest person on earth.

Until Chelsea had come back into his life.

He didn't want to be alone. Not anymore. Not ever again.

He wasn't alone.

His breath caught at the celestial vision greeting his eyes.

Chelsea stood on the balcony overlooking the sandy beach. She wore a creamy silk gown that covered her from neck to where her bare toes peeked out. The breeze blew the gown about her, plastering the fabric against her body, perfectly outlining her delectable figure.

He swallowed. Hard.

"Jared?" Her hand went to her throat, pulling the edges of her gown together. "Is that you?"

She sounded as though she thought she was imagining him.

"Were you expecting someone else?"

"I wasn't expecting you. I told you to stay away from me until you were willing to admit you have feelings for me."

Easy enough.

"I have feelings for you," he said without hesitation.

Through the shadows of the night, she stared at him. Although he knew she couldn't make out the sincerity on his face, he hoped she heard the truth in his voice, felt the truth in his presence.

Not acknowledging his admission, she walked to the edge of her balcony and leaned toward the sea. She closed her eyes and inhaled. "I love the sea. The wind, the sounds, the smell, all of it."

Jared decided right then and there that he loved the sea, too. Or perhaps it was the sea nymph on the balcony causing the palpitations in his chest rather than the waves crashing against the shore. Why wasn't she saying something about what he'd said? Was she intent on torturing him? Making him pay for his sins? Or had she realized she didn't care about him after all?

"There's something soothing about being near the water, isn't there? It's like being near it revives me," Chelsea mused without opening her eyes, embracing the wind from the Gulf. "I avoided the beach for a long time because being here made me think of you. Funny that part of the reason I came here was so I could be near you."

Jared watched her, thinking he was insane for not crossing to her and kissing her senseless, kissing her until she gasped his name and his alone.

"You revive me, Chelsea. I want you in my life."

"I'm in your life, Jared. We work together."

"That's not what I meant."

"What do you mean, Jared?" She turned, facing him again, her hair whipping around her.

"Because I'm nothing more to you than a coworker you slept with during a weak moment. We've never even been on a proper date. I'm not your girlfriend, ex or otherwise."

"No, but you should have been from the moment we met," he interrupted.

"You told me I was too young."

"You *were* too young. I hated what you did to my insides, to my supposedly well-ordered life."

"I didn't do anything to your life, Jared."

"You ripped up my definition of life, Chelsea. I had my future with Laura all mapped out in my head. Then I met you and realized I existed in black and white, that I was settling for just existing when I could have everything. You brought color into my world."

"I gave you color?" she asked, and he tired of the distance between them. He wanted to see her face clearly, to look into her eyes and know what she was feeling.

Despite her shocked protests, he wrapped his arms around her and held her arms so she couldn't pull away, held her gaze so she'd see what was in his heart.

"You gave me color. That sweet kiss you planted on my surprised lips made me see rainbows, and I've never been the same since."

Her face scrunched up, and she trembled. "Why are you saying this?"

"Because I want you to know the truth."

"I want…" She paused. "I want you to leave. I told you I can't take this anymore. By morning you'll regret having come here, and you'll go back to treating me like I have bubonic plague. I can't deal with that anymore, Jared. I won't."

"I won't leave, Chelsea. Not unless you say you don't love me anymore. But know this— leaving you isn't what I want."

"What is it you want, Jared? Because, heaven help me, I've tried to figure that out for weeks and I still don't know."

"I want you, Chelsea."

Chelsea stared at Jared and wondered what she was supposed to say. Was she supposed to graciously accept that for now he wanted her so she should make herself available once again?

What if he only let her close when his emotions were raw, like they'd been on the night Connie had died? Like they were tonight because of seeing some of the old gang he and Laura had hung out with?

Regardless of how she felt about him, she refused to let him use her that way. If nothing else, her ordeal with him had convinced her she deserved better. Much better.

Scars and all, she was lovable.

Only Jared wasn't capable of loving. Not when his heart belonged to a dead woman. She wouldn't spend the rest of her life trying to live up to a beloved memory.

"That's too bad because I no longer want you." Not when she'd only have to give him up when he'd gotten whatever he'd come for, not when she'd be left begging for his love and have to face seeing him at the clinic knowing she loved him and would never really have him.

Surprise came into his eyes, and his throat worked. "I've lost you."

Had he thought she'd just fall into his arms and welcome him into her bed after he'd ignored her since the last time he'd shown up at her doorstep?

Of course he had. For weeks she'd allowed him to walk all over her heart. Why would he expect any thing different now?

"You never had me to lose, Jared," she pointed out. "You pushed me away each and every time I tried to give myself to you."

"I was a fool."

"Yes." She wanted to look away from him but was trapped by his eyes. She could almost believe him, could almost think he believed what he was saying.

"I never deserved you," he admitted.

"You didn't," she agreed, having a harder and harder time maintaining her resolve. How could she resist him when he looked at her with such sincerity in his eyes? When she imagined she saw love in his blue gaze?

But hadn't he been wonderful the night they'd

made love? Hadn't he made her feel special, loved? She'd gone to sleep that night believing deep in her heart that Jared loved her as much as she loved him and he'd eventually realize that.

She'd been a fool, but no more.

"Forgive me, Chelsea. Give me a chance to prove things can work between us."

If he hadn't been holding her arms, Chelsea knew she'd be pinching herself because she had to be dreaming. Had to be. Then again, knowing he wouldn't feel the same come light of day made his words a cruel joke, a nightmare.

"What if things don't work, Jared?" She was playing devil's advocate. "What if we try and things get really nasty and it spills over to the clinic? What then?"

"Then we'll know for certain we gave it our best try and that I can live with. What I've discovered I can't live with is not having tried at all."

Chelsea felt her heart melting, felt her resolve cracking. Dear Lord, she needed a pinch to convince herself this was real, that Jared was saying all the things she wanted to hear.

Well, almost all the things she wanted to hear.

He hadn't said he loved her.

She wouldn't settle for less. Not about something this important.

Neither was she willing to let him keep hurting her, rejecting her just when hope entered her heart.

She hardened her heart and stared into his eyes. "Then go away knowing you tried and failed, because I'm no longer willing to have a relationship with you. We're coworkers, nothing more."

Jared deserved every barb she threw his way. Deserved the pain and more. But despite what spewed from her mouth, her eyes told a different story.

She wanted to believe him, but was afraid of being hurt yet again.

He couldn't bear her pain, to think he'd caused her so much already and held the power to cause her more. Was she right? Were they fated to be never more than coworkers?

Not even that because he couldn't bear to see her every day, to be reminded of what a fool he'd been when she'd offered her heart on a platter.

"I'll go, Chelsea. If you're sure that's what you want, but not until you know what happened all those years ago."

She didn't speak, just turned to stare out at the sea.

Jared bent, kissed her cheek, and let her go. "I loved Laura and I always will. If she hadn't died, I would have married her and found a way to be happy. But I've never felt the way I feel about you. Not about Laura or anyone else." He took a deep breath. "I knew something special had happened between us that week, that you were special. The night you kissed me, I made the decision that I was going to break things off with Laura and as soon as you turned eighteen I'd call, ask to visit you over the summer." He closed his eyes, took a deep breath, then continued. "But when I got back to med school, Laura had an announcement of her own. She was pregnant."

Chelsea's sharply indrawn breath told him what he already knew. Will had never told his sister the dirty secret behind his engagement. Only a handful of people had known.

"I never knew."

"Only a few people did. She'd discovered her condition while she was in Europe and her parents guessed the truth. The moment she told me we were going to be parents, everything changed. I asked her to marry me and pushed any feelings I had for you out of my heart. At least, I tried to. Instead, Laura realized I'd changed and it caused a rift between us. We'd argued the night she crashed." He sighed. "Foolishly, I made a vow at her funeral that I'd never let anyone else have my heart. The craziest part is that someone else already had my heart. You."

Chelsea shivered and although the warm wind whipped at them, he knew his revelation had caused her alarmed reaction. Regardless, he wasn't going to leave until he told her everything.

"I thought caring for you was dishonoring Laura. Instead, I've dishonored her by locking my heart away. For so long I thought I couldn't be with you because of how you made me feel. The way you make me feel is why I should have been by your side all along." He brushed his fingers along her cheek. "I love you, Chelsea. With all my heart and all I am. I've made so many mistakes that I don't blame you for no longer wanting me, but you've always had my heart."

He turned and walked down the steps, but instead of going to his car he headed onto the beach toward where she'd exposed her back and her heart. He'd walk until his head cleared, or until he didn't have the strength to take another step.

He took off his socks and shoes, rolled up the legs of his pants, and squished sand still warm from the day's hot sun between his toes.

That's what he'd do. Win Chelsea's trust. Win her love.

Because he could make things right and wouldn't turn his back without a fight.

Even if it took him the rest of his life, he'd spend every day proving to her that she was what mattered most to him.

"Jared!"

At first he thought the wind and waves were playing tricks on him because he was near where they'd stood just a couple of weeks ago. But when he heard her cry out his name again, he realized Chelsea had followed him onto the beach.

He turned, saw her racing toward him with her gown plastered to her.

"Wait," she called. Breathless when she caught up, she stared up at him, her face illuminated in the moonlight. "Did you mean what you said?"

"That I love you?"

Her hand pressed to her heaving chest, she nodded.

"With all my heart."

"You're sure you won't feel differently in the morning? That you're not going to take one look at me and realize you made a mistake? That you don't love me after all?"

"I love you and want you in my life. Always. My mistake has been in not telling you every moment since we met how much you mean to me."

"Then…" she placed her hands on his cheeks "…yes."

"Yes?" What was she agreeing to?

"Yes, I love you. You know I do. I always have."

Jared's chest swelled with relief and so much emotion he thought he might burst. He placed his hands on hers. He couldn't not touch her, to prove to himself she really stood before him, looking like a sea sprite and saying she loved him.

"You're willing to forgive me for all my mistakes? To marry me and spend your life with me?" he asked.

Chelsea's eyes widened, glinting in the moonlight. "You want to marry me?"

Did she think he'd settle for less than everything? He wanted the world to know she was his.

"I'll make mistakes, probably ones every bit as colossal as the ones I've made up to this point, but I love you, Chelsea. I want to spend the rest of my life showing you how much you mean to me, showing you how much I want your love, and making up for all the hurt in the past. That is, if you're willing to take a chance on me."

She leaned into him, her breath hot against his lips. "A thousand chances, if that's what it takes for us to get it right."

MEDICAL™

Large Print

Titles for the next six months…

December

SINGLE DAD SEEKS A WIFE	Melanie Milburne
HER FOUR-YEAR BABY SECRET	Alison Roberts
COUNTRY DOCTOR, SPRING BRIDE	Abigail Gordon
MARRYING THE RUNAWAY BRIDE	Jennifer Taylor
THE MIDWIFE'S BABY	Fiona McArthur
THE FATHERHOOD MIRACLE	Margaret Barker

January

VIRGIN MIDWIFE, PLAYBOY DOCTOR	Margaret McDonagh
THE REBEL DOCTOR'S BRIDE	Sarah Morgan
THE SURGEON'S SECRET BABY WISH	Laura Iding
PROPOSING TO THE CHILDREN'S DOCTOR	Joanna Neil
EMERGENCY: WIFE NEEDED	Emily Forbes
ITALIAN DOCTOR, FULL-TIME FATHER	Dianne Drake

February

THEIR MIRACLE BABY	Caroline Anderson
THE CHILDREN'S DOCTOR AND THE SINGLE MUM	Lilian Darcy
THE SPANISH DOCTOR'S LOVE-CHILD	Kate Hardy
PREGNANT NURSE, NEW-FOUND FAMILY	Lynne Marshall
HER VERY SPECIAL BOSS	Anne Fraser
THE GP'S MARRIAGE WISH	Judy Campbell

⊚™ MILLS & BOON®
Pure reading pleasure™

1108 LP 2P P1 Medical

MEDICAL™

Large Print

March

SHEIKH SURGEON CLAIMS HIS BRIDE Josie Metcalfe
A PROPOSAL WORTH WAITING FOR Lilian Darcy
A DOCTOR, A NURSE: A LITTLE MIRACLE Carol Marinelli
TOP-NOTCH SURGEON, PREGNANT NURSE Amy Andrews
A MOTHER FOR HIS SON Gill Sanderson
THE PLAYBOY DOCTOR'S MARRIAGE Fiona Lowe
PROPOSAL

April

A BABY FOR EVE Maggie Kingsley
MARRYING THE MILLIONAIRE DOCTOR Alison Roberts
HIS VERY SPECIAL BRIDE Joanna Neil
CITY SURGEON, OUTBACK BRIDE Lucy Clark
A BOSS BEYOND COMPARE Dianne Drake
THE EMERGENCY DOCTOR'S Molly Evans
CHOSEN WIFE

May

DR DEVEREUX'S PROPOSAL Margaret McDonagh
CHILDREN'S DOCTOR, Meredith Webber
MEANT-TO-BE WIFE
ITALIAN DOCTOR, SLEIGH-BELL BRIDE Sarah Morgan
CHRISTMAS AT WILLOWMERE Abigail Gordon
DR ROMANO'S CHRISTMAS BABY Amy Andrews
THE DESERT SURGEON'S SECRET SON Olivia Gates

MILLS & BOON®
Pure reading pleasure™

1108 LP 2P P2 Medical